A

BOLD,

RAW,

ROUSING CHRONICLE

of wild years and wild men—plains

Indians, buffalo hunters, border

people whose conflicts erupted into

a bitter struggle between honor

and survival . . .

The Appaloosa

by Robert MacLeod

FAWCETT GOLD MEDAL • NEW YORK

THE APPALOOSA

Published by Fawcett Gold Medal Books,
a unit of CBS Publications,
the Consumer Publishing Division of CBS Inc.

ISBN: 0-449-13971-9

The buffalo hunters, army officers and Indians
mentioned by name at the Adobe Walls battle are
historical characters, except Matt Fletcher,
Karl Koch, and Buff Akins; these three and all
others are fictional.

Printed in the United States of America

14   13   12   11   10   9   8   7   6

To Ruthie and Hod

The Appaloosa

Chapter 1

JUNE, 1874, in the Texas Panhandle. The dust and powder smoke eddied around the three closely grouped one-room sod buildings of the big buffalo camp—the store, the blacksmith shop and Hanrahan's saloon. The receding sound of the bare hoofs of five hundred Indian war-ponies still rolled across the flatness of sage and buffalo grass, and already buzzards were gathering to drop down in slow spirals.

Matt Fletcher took time to be scared.

Inside the one-room soddy, powder smoke hung in acrid layers thick enough to hide the pole rafters. Matt sneezed and swabbed his burning eyes with a greasy buckskin sleeve. He eased back on his haunches, aware now of the ache of thigh and calf muscles strained by the awkward squat he had maintained for ten minutes.

His bruised right shoulder would be turning purple where the butt of the Sharps had hammered it when he took that first hurried shot before he was set for it. He could hardly hear Karl Koch's cackling laugh because the near-intolerable racket of two buffalo guns, two Winchester '73s and two Colt .44s in the confined space, had battered his ear drums.

"Must've been five hundred of them sons," Karl said.

Buff Akins asked, "How you figure that, Karl? You count 'em?" He spat and put a bright primer on the nipple of his percussion gun.

Matt pulled the sixteen pounds of Sharps rifle back through the hole he had hacked in the two-foot sod wall fifteen minutes earlier—the rifle that could knock a man kicking at a thousand yards, and drop a bull buffalo in its tracks at five hundred.

Koch slapped him on the shoulder. "Always said next to me you was the best damn snap-shot at a runnin' target I ever seen, Matt. You sure counted coup on that buck with the medicine shield!"

Koch stooped to peer through Matt's gun hole. "Looks like his face is blowed away. Pony's layin' all over him."

Matt stood up. "If you don't shut up," he said, "I'm gonna give you the butt of this gun right in the teeth!" He walked across the room and sat beside Billy Tyler, who was reloading his Winchester, sliding the fifteen snub-nosed cartridges into the loading gate.

Koch's face put on a caricature of injured innocence. "Now what the hell did I say!" he shrugged elaborately. "Hey, Buff, you see me nail that Comanch'? He was a good hundred yards off an' goin' away like his tail's on fire, but ol' Karl sure nailed him!"

Akins ignored him. "Them Shadler boys, they're gone," he said. "I heard 'em screechin' out in their freight rig, after them Comanch' hit us. I told 'em they're crazy not to sleep inside. Said they had a lot of gear in the wagon, an' wanted to guard their mules. Now the Comanch' got the Shadlers *an'* the gear *an'* the mules!"

Bat Masterson, youngest man in the buffalo camp, said, "One minute I'm drinkin' coffee an' peekin' out to see if the sun is up, an' the next everybody's knockin' holes in the walls an' lettin' fly. Where'd all those hostiles come from?"

Matt had heard Masterson doing his shooting with the two new-fangled centerfire Colts with which he was so expert.

"They're stirred up 'cause we come down here an' crossed the Arkansas an' built this set-up," he explained. "We're breakin' the Medicine Lodge treaty, you know that. Ain't supposed to be no white hunters in the Panhandle. Quanah Parker was leadin' that charge. Takes a half-breed to really hate a white man."

"Well, they sure meant business," old Akins put in. "Never seen so many bucks all at once an' all mad. Never seen 'em keep comin' right onto the guns like that, neither. Most always, they'll split an' circle, or give it up if they're takin' a whippin'."

"You suppose the folks are all right in those other soddies?" Masterson asked. "I'll take a sashay over an' find out."

Akins said, "Go right ahead, son, if your medicine's strong. When some dead buck r'ars up behind a dead pony an' blows a hole through your lights, I'll set here thinkin' up nice things to say when we plant you."

Everyone was talkative—perhaps a reaction to the release from battle pressure. Billy Tyler said, "I was in the saloon when they hit us. I cut an' run for here, 'cause I seen Matt an' Karl an' Buff headin' for this soddy. Figured I better be with the experts. Charlie Rath an' Hanrahan was herdin' Mrs. Olds into the soddy across from the store. Bill Olds come right behind 'em, runnin' out of the blacksmith shop. Damn good thing we was up all night fixin' that busted ridgepole in the saloon. If they'd've caught the camp sleepin' . . ."

"Biggest war party I ever seen," Akins said. "Mostly Comanch', but I seen a couple 'Rapahoe, an' there was 'Pache an' Cheyenne, too. They're some riled."

"Yeh," Matt said. "Likely some medicine man made 'em all bullet proof. Can't figure no other reason they'd keep comin' even when the ponies started goin' down. I don't figure they're through yet."

Koch got a bullet mold and a bar of lead out of his war bag. "I figure the same," he said. He looked around the crowded soddy—the pile of hides in one corner and the jumble of saddles and gear strewn about. "Now, what can I build me a little fire with? Guess it's gotta be that packsaddle. Anybody got a skillet, so's I can melt this galena?"

He picked up the packsaddle, squatted companionably beside Matt, and began to whittle shavings for his fire. He shoved back his limp-brimmed wool hat, exposing the sweaty baldness. The peltry of curly brown whiskers that concealed his square face—all but the broad nose, bulging, pale eyes and wrinkled forehead—split apart in a yellow-toothed grin. He winked at Billy Tyler and said, "Now, Matt, you an' Buff bein' the Injun experts, you might say, now I was wonderin' about that Cheyenne with the medicine shield, the one you drilled clean through his pony an' all . . ."

Abruptly, Matt rose and crossed the room to sit by himself. Koch grinned and nudged Billy Tyler with his elbow. Old Akins said, "Karl, quit pushin' at him! He feels bad. You wouldn't savvy."

"Makes his livin' killin' buffalo," Koch said, "but after a stand he goes out an' wastes ca'tridges at two-bits a throw, knockin' off the orphan calves. Don't make no sense. Wolves get 'em 'fore you're out of sight."

Matt Fletcher felt bad, all right. There was a sick lump in his belly. The Cheyenne lying out there with the medicine shield and no face was his friend, Hohs Tai Wut, Spots on His Feathers. Matt had often got drunk with him on snakehead whiskey and had lost ponies to the fierce old man at the moccasin game. When he had been living with the Cheyennes, Matt had even been figuring on getting together ten ponies, the price of Spots on His Feathers' daughter.

Then Stone Calf had brought his family into the Cheyenne lodge circle and Matt had seen Stone Calf's daughter, Wo Ista, the Buffalo Woman. After that, he couldn't see any of the other dark-eyed girls who giggled and all but asked him to throw his blanket over their heads. Old Spots on His Feathers had accepted Matt's change of heart philosophically—he had even helped Stone Calf set the price for Wo Ista, and a steep price it was.

At one of the makeshift gun ports, Koch raised a yell. "Here they come ag'in!"

He slid the barrel of his Sharps out through the hole. A shot or two sounded from the other buildings. Matt knelt at his hole. Billy Tyler and Buff Akins and Masterson ran across the room.

Only two Cheyennes were riding out from the bluffs a mile away to which the horde had retreated. They came side by side, quirting the ponies at every jump.

Karl Koch grinned and cuddled his cheek against the stock of the Sharps. "Come on, you glory hunters! Come on, you settin' ducks! Just keep acomin'!"

Matt lunged for the big man, grabbed his collar with both hands and hurled him back. Koch rolled over, came up squatting and reached for the Sharps he had dropped. Matt stood on it. He reversed his own Sharps and held it like a club.

"Leave 'em go, Karl," he said.

Old Akins suddenly bellowed through the doorway to the hunters in the other buildings, "Quit shootin'! You, Charlie Rath, Hanrahan, Olds! Don't shoot!"

Koch squatted, glaring at Matt. A few shots roared from the adjoining soddy, then there was only the sound of drumming hoofs on the turf.

Akins called back from the window, "They picked him off'n the ground arunnin', Matt. Two big coup-feathers for them bucks, come next Sun Dance!"

Matt stepped away from Koch's rifle and looked through his gun port to watch the two bucks ride away with Spots on His Feathers' body flopping limply across the withers of a war pony.

Koch sighed and stood up. "I declare, Matt, sometimes

. . . Who the hell's side are you on?" He picked up a handful of dirt and flung it down savagely.

"Karl," Matt said, "they wasn't fixin' to hurt no one, just pickin' up their dead. If somebody scalps that warrior, he never does get to see the Camp Circle of the Gods."

Muttering, Karl Koch squatted by a small fire and poured bright liquid lead into a bullet mold.

With toothless gums, Buff Akins worried a chaw from a twist of tobacco and dribbled tobacco juice down his beard. He ran a cleaning rag through the bore of the percussion gun, then dumped a small handful of black powder into the muzzle. He set the ball on the greased patch and with one smooth motion, rammed it home. He said, "We better keep an eye out. Them medicine men an' Dog Soldiers had time to get 'em fired up ag'in. Matt, you think it's just buffalo that's got 'em so warlike?"

"That's it," Matt said. "They know the northern herd's all gone. There ain't no more buffalo, so to speak, exceptin' down here south of the Arkansas. We're the first whites that jumped the line. They know what it means if all them hunters an' skinners follows us down here. They're likely to hang around for weeks an' let nobody out of here. This ain't no flash raid for horses. Might be a good idea to take our foot in our hand and move out."

Masterson practiced quick draws, first the right-hand Colt, then the left. "How you goin' to get out of here with Injuns thicker'n lice in a blanket?" he asked.

"Can be done at night," Akins replied. "They stick to their camps then—there's demons around looking for Injun souls after sundown. Feller could walk out quiet an' easy an' not leave no sign, an' wade the creek for a mile or two an' git away. But you'd have to put a lot of space behind you by mornin'."

Koch cut the sprues from the new slugs and carefully wrapped the paper patches around the butt ends before seating them in the cases. "I say stick here an' cut 'em down. The more we cut down, the quicker we get back to makin' hides."

"How come you got a right to them buffalo, Karl?" Matt asked. "You can go prospectin' or take up a homestead or grab you a cattle spread up in Montana on Injun land—you got a lot of ways to make a livin'. Injuns got nothin' but buffalo. It's either that or starve on some reservation an' get robbed by the agents. How would you like it?"

"Goddamn!" Koch hurled the bullet mold into a corner. "You a white man or a dirty buck, Matt? Sometimes I wonder! You got the black hair an' the mud-color skin, all except them little piggy green eyes. How come you're runnin' off to them Cheyenne camps every chance you get? How come you're arguin' their side all the time? That Cheyenne bitch, Buffalo Woman or whatever, she had you horsin' around after her like a stud! Is that it, or are you a stinkin' breed yourself? I've knowed you in a lot of camps an' I never could figure you out!"

Slowly Matt stood up, his thumb on the hammer of the Sharps. Bat Masterson skipped nimbly from behind Koch and walked over to lean against the far wall.

"So if I am?" Matt asked.

"Now you boys quit it!" Akins demanded. "Ain't we got enough trouble? Set down, Matt!"

Far away sounded the garbled notes of a bugle.

"Hey! Cavalry!" Tyler yelled and ran to his gun port.

Buff Akins stuffed six rifle balls into his mouth and mumbled around them, "That's Injun. Some buck's got him a bugle an' prob'ly some pony-soldier hair to go with it." He poured a handful of powder into his shirt pocket to have it ready for rapid fire. He sat down carefully at his gun hole and wiggled his skinny buttocks for a comfortable fit on the dirt floor.

The long line of mounted warriors charged through waves of ground heat. The bugle blatted again, quavering crazily. Fast ponies began to show out ahead of the line. A thin, high squalling came faintly, swelling louder. Trade muskets and a few repeating rifles began to fire too soon from the charging line, and there was the deep-throated boom of one buffalo gun.

Matt yelled, "Pick off them ones out in front, where the rest can see 'em drop!"

He pushed the aperture of the sight vane up to the two-hundred yard mark, and lined up on the chest of a gray pony, deliberately choosing the mount instead of the rider, a screaming old man who sat straight up and brandished a coup lance which fluttered with eagle feathers.

The recoil banged against his sore shoulder. Through the rolling white smoke he saw the pony somersault, two hundred yards away, and the rider hit rolling. Unhurt, the warrior scrambled for the shelter of his dead mount.

Buff Akins' percussion gun bellowed and a pony fell, then struggled up with a foreleg dangling. Its rider slashed its throat with a skinning knife, kicked its good leg out from under it and flung himself behind it when it dropped.

To his left, Matt heard Billy Tyler's '73 blasting steadily like a piece of machinery. At the far wall, Bat Masterson's rifle spoke at irregular intervals. Not many attackers headed around the building toward Masterson's side. As the range shortened, Matt had no time to adjust the sight, but compensated by holding lower.

The charging line swept up to the buildings, whirled around and between them. There was a crescendo of firing from the three occupied buildings, and a confusion of yelling. A bullet kicked dirt into Matt's eyes and a war arrow whipped through his gun hole and drove quivering into the floor.

He ground powder-grimed knuckles into his eyes and blinked through the tears and the smoke. The attack had faltered and become a retreat.

Only Karl Koch kept firing, as fast as he could reload—five evenly spaced, careful shots—before the Indians drew out of range. Three riders, shot in the back, plummeted to earth, where one lay stretched out, slowly drawing up one knee again and again until Koch shot him through the head at two hundred yards. The other two lay as they had fallen, unmoving.

Matt wanted to slug Koch on the head. He said nothing.

When his pulse quit hammering and his vision cleared, he borrowed Billy Tyler's Winchester.

"How's it hold, Billy?" he asked.

" 'Bout two inches left at a hundred yards," Tyler answered. "Won't reach two hundred yards flat. If you got some far-off target spotted, you better use your Sharps."

"This'll do me," Matt said. He shoved the sight forward one notch.

There was a pony out there, sitting on its haunches like a big dog, running a thin stream of blood from its mouth. Matt shot it through the head and levered another shell into the chamber.

Eagerly, Karl Koch peered over Matt's shoulder and cocked

his Sharps. "What you got, boy? Some cripples out there? Don't be no dog-in-the-manger now, show me!"

A pony lay on its side, struggling to raise its head. Matt shot it.

"You Goddamn' fool!" Koch seized Matt's arm and jerked him back. "Goddamn you, Matt! You crazy? Them's good car'ridges you're wastin'! We'll be fightin' here maybe a month! I oughta bust your head!"

"Get your hands off, Karl!"

Matt jacked another shell into the chamber. "There's wounded bucks out there. Don't cut loose at none of them, I'm tellin' you! An' keep your hands off me!"

He knelt and looked out. There were surprisingly few dead Indians, but many dead ponies lay there, looking oddly deflated. Nothing moved except a single warrior who kept raising himself on his arms like a man doing exercises. Matt could hear him singing. He was too far away to hear the words, but Matt knew it was the warrior's death song, imploring the Grandfathers to guide his moccasins straight on the Hanging Trail in the Sky.

Two warriors came riding side by side from the foot of the distant bluff, heading at full gallop for the wounded man.

Matt handed the Winchester to Billy Tyler. "Thanks, Billy."

Slowly, Matt cleaned the big buffalo gun. He shoved the 525-grain bullet into the breech and snapped the lever shut. He walked across to where Koch stood glowering at him.

"Karl," he said, "shootin' orphan calves an' crippled ponies maybe looks crazy to you. Maybe you got a right to be sore. But crippled Injuns, that's somethin' else. What the hell does it get you to murder 'em?"

"Sweet Jesus! Wasn't they tryin' to murder *me?*" Koch snarled.

"Not when they're goin' the other way, or layin' out there bleedin' to death. Listen, Karl, they'll get tired of this—they ain't gettin' nowhere. Just stand 'em off. What's the use to gun 'em down if we don't have to?"

"You all through?" Sarcasm was heavy in Koch's voice.

"Not yet, Karl."

Matt stepped back a pace. "Just before this last set-to, you was sayin' maybe I'm Injun. I'm curious. S'pose I was nigger, or Mex. You feel the same about them?"

"For God sakes, what is this? Some debatin' society?"

"Not quite," Matt said. "If you wanta know my real name, it ain't Matt—it ain't even Matthew. It's Mateo. I could give myself the full handle an' say it's Mateo Frederick Fletcher y Gómez. My ma was half Mex'can. Now, you're a Texan, an' I know how you feel about Mex'cans—they're lower than dirt. I talked Spanish 'fore I talked English, an' I got full-blood Mex'can cousins an' uncles an' all that. I never figured you was touchy about half-bloods, or Injun blood or Mex'can, or I'd've told you."

"What the hell you tellin' me now for?"

"Just givin' you your say, Karl. If you wanta do somethin', now's the time."

Koch spat a foul word and walked away to sit on a pile of buffalo hides. For several minutes there was an uneasy silence.

"What're we goin' to do about eatin'?" Bat Masterson asked.

Buff Akins relaxed. "I'll go over an' git somethin', soon as it's dark," he said.

The third attack came about four in the afternoon. Not more than forty warriors charged from the shelter of the bluff. Ready at the gun ports, the five hunters waited in silence for them to come within range.

Suddenly Akins warned, "Now, look! This'n' might be the worst. Them's Cheyenne Dog Soldiers an' a few Comanch', real do-or-die boys. They're after coups, an' they'll die tryin' to get 'em. So let 'em have it good!"

It was execution, methodical and efficient.

From the three sod houses came a steady roll of fire. Ponies and warriors began to drop at two hundred yards, but the rest came on at a pounding gallop, screeching their battle shouts. Not ten of them reached the buildings. Akins threw the door open and shot one so close that the warrior rolled half inside and died gasping in the doorway.

Matt fired as fast as he could reload, and he missed only once. He shot no ponies this time.

The firing slackened. A warrior screamed in agony out in front until Koch killed him.

Suddenly Masterson, at the rear wall, yelled, "Watch out! One comin' round the corner!"

Next to the corner, Billy Tyler tried to angle his rifle to bear. A lance-head flashed through his gun port and jabbed into his stomach.

Matt swung his Sharps sideways, but could see only the

rump of a frantic, leopard-spotted pony. He scrambled on his knees to Tyler's side and shoved the rifle out. The lance rammed through again, glanced off his rifle barrel and thrust deep into Billy Tyler's chest. Tyler screamed, grabbed it and fell backward. Deeply imbedded, the lance came with him and stood up, gyrating.

Matt tipped the Sharps up and, at point-blank range, shot the warrior in the belly. He heard the man's gagging grunt and the squeal of the pony.

When the smoke blew away, he saw the warrior topple slowly and fall heavily. The body, with one shoulder still caught in the loop of horsehair rope braided into the pony's mane to support a side-riding warrior, dragged bumping beside the pony. The spotted pony swung around and came to a halt like a keel boat bringing up at anchor.

Billy Tyler retched and died. There was a lot of blood.

It was as though the world held its breath, no shots, no words spoken—even the wind had stopped. Only the bare hoofs of the pony tethered to the dead warrior made a little drumming dance.

Karl Koch shrugged, jerked the lance free and tossed it through the doorway. He caught up Billy Tyler's hands and dragged him into a corner where he wrapped him in a hide and rolled him against the wall.

Matt started to speak, but nothing came out. He tried again—"Buff, cover me, will you?"

He laid his rifle down and walked out through the doorway, stepping over the dead warrior.

The spotted pony reared and almost pulled free before he got his hands on the trailing jaw-rein with its stretched scalp and the two hawk feathers, knotted under the pony's chin. When he drew his skinning knife and cut the hair rope in which the warrior's body was caught, the pony squealed and plunged, dragging Matt so that his heels dug furrows in the sod.

Then Buff Akins was out, beating the pony's rump with his rifle barrel. Matt dragged on the jaw-rein. Somehow, they bullied and fought the little horse to the soddy, where Akins kicked it. It lunged through the doorway, snorting at the dead Comanche.

Matt caught up a forefoot, shoved with his shoulder and threw the little stallion. He managed to hogtie its thrashing feet.

Akins leaned against the wall until he got his breath, then said, "Matt, give me a hand. There's a lineback dun out there, just creased across the butt. A dead buck's tangled in the rein."

The dun was a little easier than the spotted horse, but it took ten minutes to haul and hammer it through the doorway. Not until it was thrown and hogtied did Matt pay attention to Koch's rage.

Koch, his face red, was almost screaming.

"You *crazy*, you two? What the hell *is* this! Get 'em outa here! Get 'em out!"

He squatted to untie the spotted stallion.

Matt picked up Tyler's Winchester. He worked the lever. The breech opened with a click, and the empty case flipped over his shoulder. The fresh cartridge snapped into place. He put the butt against his sore shoulder and aimed at Koch's head.

"Get away from that pony," he said.

It must have been a half-minute before Koch stood up. He kept staring into Matt's eyes.

"By God," he said softly, "I think you would!"

Chapter 2

CHARLES RATH came into the soddy.

"How you boys make out? I think that last charge was the big finolly!" He grinned; but his lean face sobered swiftly when he saw the blood and the hide-wrapped bundle in the corner. His eyes took swift census.

"Billy Tyler!"

"He got a lance in the belly," Akins said.

"Guess we're lucky at that," Rath said. "Too bad—nice kid. Good hunter, too. Have to plant him pretty soon, this hot weather an' all."

"Anybody git hurt over there?" Akins asked.

"Not a scratch. I been over to the storehouse, too. Nobody got hurt. Came over to tell you Mrs. Olds is boilin' up some tongues. Got biscuits fired up too, an' I'm puttin' out canned peaches, courtesy of Rath and Wright. You boys come over one at a time. What you think, Buff? I figure this is about played out, but we'll keep our eye peeled an' stay inside. They'll be sneakin' around tryin' pot shots for weeks."

"Seems like," Akins said.

"Army'll get word," Rath said. "This sort of shindig gets around. They'll come down from Fort Supply an' bail us out. Liable to be a little wrathy 'bout our bein' here. Well, we'll just set tight till they get here. Don't anybody go pirootin' around outside and get in trouble, hear?"

He had not overlooked the two ponies lying quiet and uncomfortable against the end wall.

"Looks like a couple of you figure on pullin' out," he said. "Good lookin' stud, that Appaloosa. Who, you an' Matt?" he asked Akins.

At Akins' nod, he said, "Yeh, I thought so. Guess it don't matter. I think this place is finished." He grinned and walked out.

As soon as Rath had gone, Koch said plaintively, "Matt, look! I don't wanta start no trouble—we been friends—but for sweet God's sake, just tell me! Here we got a stack of green hides stinkin' in the corner already. Billy Tyler, there, he's gonna start stinkin' by noon tomorrow, an' I ain't got no plans to plant him out there tonight, with them hostiles huntin' hair. We gotta sit cooped up here, how long? Ten days? Two weeks? An' now you two haul them ponies in here. We're gonna have horseshit up to our knees!" His voice rose. "Matt . . ."

"Git the kink out'n your tail, boy," Akins said. "I'll tell you what Matt's thinkin'. The Army's bound to come down. We're breakin' the law, an' them colonels ain't gonna laugh this off—might be the start of a big outbreak. We might wind up in the jug. So why sit around an' wait?"

He cocked a bushy eyebrow at Matt, who nodded.

"Git on with it, Buff," Karl said.

"Now, where you s'pose that cayuse of yours is, an' them four mules for your hide wagon? They're Injun ponies now, if they ain't et up already. They ain't a horse left in this camp, except them two layin' there."

"You try ridin' out of here an' you'll lose what little hair you got left," Koch insisted. "I wouldn't try it for all Rath's money!"

"You wouldn't make it if you *did* try," Akins said. "You

think with a gun 'stead of your head. We'll muffle them ponies' feet an' lead 'em in the water down to the South Fork past Ol' 'Dobe Walls. Then we wade down the river an' just keep goin'.'"

One at a time, the four hunters went to Rath's soddy to eat, and returned.

Matt and Akins untied the ponies and let them stand. Matt spent some time soothing the Appaloosa stud. There were two red handprints, one each side of the stallion's neck, to indicate that its owner had ridden down enemies in battle. Painted hoofprints, hard to distinguish among the dollar-size black spots on the white rump, boasted of stolen horses. There was a red, zig-zag lightning mark painted on the muscular chest, and each big eye was ringed with blue paint to help the horse to see in the dark.

A small beaded buckskin bag was tied to a strand of mane. Buff Akins backed away with something like fear in his eyes when Matt took it off. It contained the Cheyenne warrior's secret powerful medicine.

Matt untied the battle-knot in the sparse Appaloosa tail. The horse was still snorty, but it permitted him to pet it, and seemed to listen when he talked quietly to it.

Akins' dun fought him when he rubbed grease into the bullet crease on its rump. He made a twitch of a rawhide thong and twisted it onto the pony's upper lip. Thereafter, it stood rolling its eyes, but did not move, while Matt held the twitch taut and Akins finished greasing the wound.

Akins said, "This 'n's pure jughead Injun cayuse, but you know what you got there, Matt—that split ear an' all?"

"I know," Matt replied.

Masterson asked, "What's special about that stud? He won't go more'n fourteen hands."

Akins looked disgusted. "Well, first off, look how he's put together—cannons straight as a ramrod, big deep chest, big forearms, nice hard gaskins an' a big, gentle eye. That's just what your eye tells you. What them spots an' that split ear tells you is somethin' else. This is a Nez Percé buffalo horse from way up in Idyho. He won't never step on a rope, even in a stampede. He'll put you alongside a buffalo cow in just the right spot to shove a lance under her short ribs. He'll guide by your knees, an' he'll keep fat where a cayuse wouldn't even find no graze. Any Comanch' will give you ten ponies an' three, four squaws for this one, an' figure he's out-traded you. They split one ear so's you can feel it in the dark an' won't rope him out for no *travois* haulin' or squaw work."

As soon as old man Akins quit holding forth about the qualities of the Appaloosa stallion, Koch said, "Matt, after lecturin' me all afternoon about what's the point of killin' Injuns, you didn't mind blowin' the belly off that Cheyenne that stuck the lance into Billy Tyler. How about explainin' me the difference between you shootin' 'em an' me shootin' 'em?"

"Why'n't you shut your Goddamn face!" old Buff said.

Swift anger rose in Matt. He got up and walked past Koch out the door. All evening he had fought against conceding the reality of what had happened.

He sat down against the sod wall and saw again, as clear as though it were there before him, the strong, lean face of Wohk Pos Its. Not as today, screaming with lust to kill, rigid with shock when Matt's bullet took him in the belly, but a year ago, in 1873, in the big camp on Lodgepole Creek.

Wohk Pos Its, son of Stone Calf and beloved brother of Wo Ista . . . Wo Ista, the Buffalo Woman, who had come smiling, beautiful and virgin to Matt's lodge after he had paid Stone Calf the Appaloosa stallion, the Henry rifle, the ten pounds of copperwire and the two gallons of whisky.

For all his hot lust for the slim girl, it had been hard to give up the Appaloosa. Matt had bought it only a week before—had not even had time to get acquainted with it nor to think of a name for it. And he had paid so much for it that the memory still galled him—twelve good ponies, two iron kettles and a twenty-five pound bar of lead—to the grinning Hunkpapa Sioux who had probably done no more than commit murder for the buffalo horse. But the possession of the Appaloosa had raised Matt's already high prestige among the Cheyennes, and Matt was sure that nothing less than the great little stallion would have bought Wo Ista.

Now, Wohk Pos Its would rot, a hide-wrapped package on a high platform with the bones of a good pony bleaching on the ground beneath. Stone Calf would give away his lodge, his ponies, his blankets, his Henry rifle—and Wo Ista would rip her clothes, rub ashes into her clean hair, gash her legs with a skinning knife and chop off one finger at the knuckle.

Now I've killed her brother, an' I can't ever go back to my lodge an' lie against the back rest while she picks the fat pieces out of the pot for me or sits there sewin' the dyed quills onto my moccasins. Won't never again comb her hair for her in the mornin' an' paint the red stripe down the part. . . . Never again wait achin' in my guts for her to lash the cover across the lodge opening, peel her doeskin dress off, an' come onto my sleepin' platform an' turn herself loose, hot an' wild an' crazy as me.

"Buff," he said, "let's get our gear together, if you're comin'. I'm pullin' out tonight."

Just before they left, Koch shook Matt's hand in an embarrassed way.

"I'll see you some place," Matt said.

"Keep your hair on tight, Matt."

There was some trouble with the ponies at first, but a tight hitch with a lariat around each soft nose fixed that. By midnight, Matt and Akins had led them down the two miles of creek past the ruins of Old Adobe Walls, the ill-fated trading post built by Bent and St. Vrain way back in the '30s, and on down to the juncture with the South Fork of the Canadian. They had stayed in the shallow waters of the creek and had encountered no danger.

Matt did not venture to mount the spotted pony because he anticipated trouble with the little horse and its hatred of white-man smell, and because it was only prudent to lead it, ready to smother any nickering. He had his Sharps, his bullet mold, thirty loaded shells, his knife, an old Navy cap-and-ball revolver, ten pounds of jerky and a buffalo-paunch water bag. A Navajo blanket, heavy and rainproof, completed his outfit, with one exception—fifteen hundred eighty dollars in gold in a buckskin moneybelt tight about his flat-muscled middle.

They left the water at the fork of the river. Akins squatted, squeezed the water from his sagging pants legs, and pulled a stone-bowled pipe from a quill-decorated pipe bag.

He shielded the spurt of a sulphur match under his coat. When the pipe was fired up, he absent-mindedly offered the pipe stem to the Four Directions and to the Power of the Earth Below and the Power of the Wise One Above.

"What you gonna do, Matt? Keep on huntin'?"

"No, Buff. I figure buffalo is finished, except you want to go bone pickin'. I ain't sorry. I went into the war when I was seventeen. Saw a lot of killin'. Come home an' went buffalo huntin'—nothin' but more killin', stinkin' hide camps an' tongue camps, live like a dog, work like a horse, blow it every winter in some deadfall town. Throw it away across the faro table or over the bar, or upstairs in some hog ranch with a hatchet-face whore."

"You named it," Akins agreed, "but what else is there? A few played it smart, like Charlie Rath, but I couldn't never seem to get the hang of savin' a dollar. How old are you, Matt? Maybe you got time to git into some other line."

"Thirty, I figure."

"Hell, you got lots of time. Well, I tell you, I'm a Piegan man. Had two Piegan squaws, up in Montana. Never lived better. I'm goin' back up there. But, if you was to come—I know you're partial to the Cheyenne—I might stop off with you in some Cheyenne camp. Didn't you have a squaw last year? Seems like I heard . . ."

Matt broke in, "Well, don't think I better, Buff. You know, my pa left me a piece of ground down in New Mexico. He fought for Texas, went way down into Mexico. Anyways, he brought back a half-Mex'can wife, an' was gonna settle in Texas. But you know them Texans, they hate Mex'cans like poison. Didn't make no difference that my pa got his arm shot off alongside of 'em, they still made it bad for him 'cause he married my ma. So he took up this place in New Mexico."

"You goin' there?" Akins asked.

"Yeh, I guess so. Ain't seen it in four years. I got a second cousin name of Gómez an' his wife, they're pure Mex'can. We was raised together like brothers. They been livin' on the place. It ain't good for much—too hot an' too dry. But I'm kind of homesick."

"Well, if that's the way your stick floats." Akins knocked out the pipe and put it carefully into the bag. "I can still make a few miles 'fore daylight. So long, Matt."

Matt started out, keeping to the shallows of the river and, with the first hint of daylight, began to look for a place to hole up through the day. Behind him, the chunky Indian pony followed with no fuss. Matt took the hitch from its nose and tied the lariat loosely around its neck, so it would be more comfortable.

Chapter 3

IN THE NEXT three nights, Matt traveled about sixty miles west, upstream along the South Fork of the Canadian. The spotted pony led readily now, and seemed to pay attention to Matt's low-voiced discussion of any conversational topic that came into his head—talk that was intended to accustom the pony to his voice. He made no attempt to impose his will on it as yet, wanting to reach some place he considered reasonably safe before starting an argument; but he handled and petted it while he let it graze in the dawn hours, before finding a place of concealment for the day.

The pony did not spook at the sudden alarms of disturbed antelope nor the deep music of baying wolves. Its interest quickened to eagerness, however, when the smell of buffalo floated past on the soft night breeze. It always detected the big humped brutes before Matt was aware of their presence, and showed an alert readiness to be off after them.

Matt slept through the sultry heat of the days with the hobbled pony tied to his wrist, usually in the shade of a cutbank or among scrubby willows or ragged cottonwoods beside the diminishing river.

On the fourth night from Adobe Walls, instead of moving on, he lay resting and let the pony graze, moving it frequently to fresh grass so it would get a good bellyful. When daylight came, he slowly studied three hundred sixty degrees of the horizon, and saw no smoke or dust.

He led the Appaloosa to the river and let it drink until it stood splashing its head up and down, playing with the water.

"That ought to take some of the ambition out of you, that load of bunch grass an' river water. We better have this out now, so's we know where we stand."

He led the pony out of the shallows, then got his left arm over its neck, high behind the ears, and hung his weight there. He held the rein rope in his right hand and poked his thumb against the side of the pony's mouth. When it opened grudgingly, he got the rope around its jaw and made the knot.

With the small head snubbed close and a tight grip on a handful of mane, he made his attempt to mount, Indian style, from the off side, hoping that the little horse's distrust of him was, by this time, mostly bluff. But the pony squealed and lunged sideways before he was set, and he had to roll off. It dragged him a few feet, then reared, fighting the painful pull of the jaw-rein.

Matt went down the rein hand over hand, pulled the stallion's head down and grabbed the split ear. The Appaloosa quieted as he talked to it.

He led it to the coiled lariat which lay by the Navajo blanket and the big Sharps. He knotted the lariat loosely about the thick-muscled neck, then quickly, before the pony realized his intention, got the lariat around the pastern of the off hind hoof and pulled it off the ground. He hauled the hoof up against the round belly and held it there with a slip-knot at the neck loop.

Helpless on three feet, the pony could do no more than wall its eyes and snort as Matt climbed on. He took the trailing end of the twelve-foot rein, coiled it loosely, and thrust it under his belt in back. If the pony managed to pile him up, he could still grab the rein before it got away from him entirely.

"All right," Matt said, "do your damn'dest, so's you'll know who's the big chief around here!" He clamped his legs on the round barrel, pulled the rein tight, gripped the mane with his rein hand and pulled the slipknot free.

The Appaloosa went humpbacked off the ground. It landed with a thump that jarred Matt's spine and went into a series of zig-zag rail-fence pitches that were easy to anticipate and meet. Matt did not try to keep its head up nor do any fancy riding, just made sure he stayed on with his legs squeezed tight and a strong grip on the mane. He was amused that the pony, for all its attempt to act like a real bronco, managed to avoid stepping on the trailing lariat.

"You're a pure bluffer!" he grunted while his head snapped back and forth between pitches. "Never was an Appaloosa that knew how to buck!"

When he squeezed hard with his right knee, the pony responded to the signal and turned toward the river, even while it continued its crow-hop pitching. The water slowed it down. It splashed through and went into loose sand on the far side. The fetlock-deep sand gave it no solid footing, and the bucking slowed to mere token jumps of protest.

When Matt pulled the coiled rein rope from his belt, doubled it and slashed down the pony's haunch, it stopped bucking and went into a hard, straightaway run. Matt yelled into the split ear and slapped the hard neck, squeezing with his right knee at the same time. The pony took the proper lead like a polo mount and swung left. At a squeeze of the left knee, it turned sharply to the right.

"Now you done what you figured you had to," Matt said, "and showed me you wouldn't take no white man on your back without a fight. I understand. Let's quit this foolishness now, an' be friends."

The small ears twitched back, listening to his voice. For half an hour Matt put the pony through its paces—figure eights, sliding stops that furrowed the ground, sudden spurts of speed, all in instant obedience to a squeeze of the knee or a light pull on the rein.

Matt pulled it down to a walk and put it into the river again. It came out streaming water and walked without guidance to the little pile of gear on the Navajo blanket. He got off, caught up the trailing lariat and removed the jaw-rein. When he swatted the spotted rump, the pony walked away a few steps, nosed the ground, turned around twice, then flopped down with a thump and rolled four times, over and back. Grunting, it surged to its feet and began to feed.

Matt pulled up a handful of grass and walked to the pony. It paid no attention to him, but continued to graze while he rubbed down the sweated back and the wet legs. It did not so much as shift its feet when he rubbed down the cannons and around the fetlocks. He picked up the feet one by one, examining the small, rock-hard hoofs for sand cracks or stone bruises around the frogs.

Matt straightened up and scratched the broad forehead and ran his hand down the face. Gently he rubbed the velvet nose. The pony flopped its lips against his hand, then rubbed its head against his chest, thrusting hard, pushing him back a step. When Matt grasped its forelock and pulled, it followed him at once, holding its head a little to one side to keep the lariat clear of its feet.

Matt said, "Freckles, let's try something. I wanta really find out."

He snatched off his hat and flapped it in front of the pony's face. The pointed ears went up, the head tossed and the pony took one step back and looked at him.

"By God, somebody really did a job on you, some old Nez Percé horse breeder. Somebody knew how to make a horse out of you!"

He put his arms around the hard-muscled neck and hugged. "Old Spotted Ass! Ol' Freckle Face!" he said into the split ear. "You wanta go to Ojo Prieto an' get a haircut an' a new shirt an' a bath? Now you keep a sharp eye out for dust an' sign an' smoke signals, an' let me know right off if you smell Injun. I'll do the same for you."

He folded the Navajo blanket and roped it onto the pony's back and tied on the water skin and the jerky sack. He slung the cartridge bag over his shoulder, walked around to the pony's off side and mounted awkwardly because of the rifle in his hand. When he squeezed with his knees, the spotted horse stepped out, fresh and eager.

"I better start teachin' you Spanish, for when we get home —*Arre! Ándale, Pecas!*"

Pecas, the freckled pony, broke into an easy lope.

In the next two days, the Appaloosa went a hundred and forty miles and showed no sign of distress or gaunting, even on the scanty graze. Matt's graze was not so scanty, although a trifle monotonous, consisting of a saddle of an antelope doe knocked down at three hundred yards. Matt had taken the precaution of tying the rein around his waist in case the Appaloosa might prove gun-shy; but Pecas only flung his head up when the 200 grains of black powder exploded like the crack of doom, then calmly went on grazing. Matt was elated at this further evidence that a master hand had broken Pecas.

This was still Comanche country—maybe Apache, too, and Matt felt as exposed in the emptiness of prairie as a bedbug on a sheet. His alertness never flagged. He found discarded rawhide horseshoes and a worn-out peak-toed moccasin at an old fire hole, and came upon the tracks of many barefoot ponies, perhaps the war trails of raiders under last fall's Comanche moon; he saw distant dust funnels and, once, faraway smoke signals towering into the sky, but not one other human being.

The Llano Estacado was now behind, to the south and east.

They cut southwest, across the Conchas, then the Pecos, and followed the Rio Grande almost to Las Cruces, well clear of the dread Jornada del Muerto which lay between the Sacramento Mountains and the Black Range. Finally they camped one night within sight of the far, few twinkling lights that located Ojo Prieto, which was four miles from Mexico.

"We'll hit her in the mornin', fresh as a couple daisies," Matt said as he offered the pony half of the remaining water, tepid and foul when he poured it into the crown of his old wool hat. "Four years since I seen that town, Pecas. Four years of hide camps, freeze in the winter, burn in the summer, live like a Goddamn animal, risk your hair. Nothin' to show for it but fifteen hundred dollars."

The Appaloosa lifted its nose from the hat and rubbed its forehead against his chest. Matt hugged the crested, stallion neck with its scanty Appaloosa mane, and said, "Well, I got me a horse, Pecas. You ain't much for size, but I'm beginnin' to think you're the best damn mount from here to anywhere! Maybe you're worth the whole danged four years!"

He ate a scrap of antelope that had begun to smell, pulled off his mule-ear boots (one sole had begun to flap) and stretched out on the dirty, beautiful Navajo blanket.

"Wo Ista was worth it, too. That first time with her, after I managed to hold back an' not pull off her virginity rope for the four days—just that first time was worth anything a man could name. An' after that things quieted down some, an' it wasn't all just wrasslin' an' laughin' on the sleepin' platform—but just havin' her around on those huntin' trips, or grainin' hides, or hangin' meat on the jerky string. By God, there was never a mornin' in them whole two years she didn't wake up with a smile on her face!

"Then I got crazy in the head or somethin' an' got to thinkin' about the buffalo camps an' the hide wagons rollin' into Dodge, an' Ben Thompson's Bull's Head Tavern in Abilene with the big red bull painted on the front, knockers an' all. . . . An' her not sayin' nothin' while I pulled out, just lookin' at me with them black eyes when I took the money out of the pipe bag an' saddled up. Wish't I'd've gone back while I could!"

The face of Spots on His Feathers took shape in Matt's mind—half of his face . . . and Wohk Pos Its riding away, swaying like a drunkard, pitching off the pony, and the copper-tan face of Wo Ista, Buffalo Woman, her black eyes smiling, and her strong loving hands.

Matt gagged on the meat, and got up to talk to Pecas. If the town wasn't shut down, he'd ride in right now. He knew he would have no sleep this night.

Chapter 4

OJO PRIETO made a deceptively pleasing appearance from half a mile away on a windswept July morning. The adobes lining the single street were warm brown or glaring white. A new tin roof glittered like a gambler's stickpin. The cottonwoods outlining the plaza flickered silvery in the wind.

From half a mile away you couldn't see the cracks and discoloration of the adobe walls. You couldn't see the grime on the windows of McAleer's General Store, nor the dead flies around the sun-faded merchandise behind the windows, nor could you see the windrows of torn paper and rusted cans against the walls and the dead dog in the street. Your nose didn't cringe at the mustiness of dead cigars and slopped beer wafting from Daggett's saloon and the reek of sour *pulque* from the Cantina Chihuahueña.

In four years the street had extended three buildings in one direction and one in the other. Matt wouldn't stop long, just get his beard whittled off and his hair cut, buy boots and a shirt and hat and horehound candy for Paco Gómez's kids, and maybe a bottle of *mezcal* before he rode the last eight miles to the ranch.

As he rode past the first new building, a one-room adobe with a barred window and a sign that read, "Ojo Prieto Jail —City Marshal," Matt was suddenly aware of his own aroma, a compound of sweat, unwashed shirt and horse smell—the identifying aura of all buffalo men. He must look like hell in the shapeless hat, the filthy clothes, the tangled hair down to his shoulders and the black, curly beard. And without even a saddle, just a filthy Navajo blanket tied onto a split-eared Indian pony.

A tall figure lounged in the door of the marshal's shack, a figure with hair as long as Matt's under a white Stetson, chestnut hair smooth and well tended. The fringed buckskin shirt was spotless. The gambler's stripe-pants were tucked neatly into fancy-stitched boots with three-inch heels. An ivory-gripped Colt hung in a carved holster from a belt with a silver horseshoe for a buckle.

The tall man took a step forward, hooking thumbs into the shell belt. The star glittered on his left shirt-pocket. He spoke through a handlebar mustache.

"Stranger?"

"No," Matt answered, and rode on.

Town marshal, huh? That was a new one for Ojo Prieto —town must be feelin' its oats.

Matt began to catch the music of soft-spoken Spanish coming from open doorways, from loiterers who studied him with seeming indifference. He thought with pleasure of his native language; how, when a man switched from English to Spanish, he dropped the chopped-off sentences and the slang and the dirtiness, and the Spanish came out with every sentence neat and complete—even the cussing was almost polite.

Pecas stepped smartly from the narrow street into the plaza, and Matt angled the pony toward the hitchrack in front of McAleer's Store.

"We got a problem here, Pecas," he said. "Do we go into the store first, or over to Daggett's for a shot of tanglefoot, or up to Teofilo's *peluquería* for a bath an' a haircut?"

Embarrassed, he glanced around to see if anyone had heard him talking to the pony like some locoed prospector to his burro.

Near the hitchrack, a Mexican on a tall roan horse spoke to another who stood holding the braided reins of a rangy gray, and this Spanish was not so pretty.

"Lázaro, behold! This *hideputa Yanqui* with the nauseating odor rides a horse of quality, a horse with pride."

Matt rode on, turning his head for a thorough inspection of the two, but refraining from answering the insult.

The man who had spoken—slim, brown, young—returned his stare with arrogance. He sat an elegant Mexican saddle, its tree covered with white rawhide, its roping horn as big as a child's head. He wore the cruel Mexican rowels of six long points on the heels of flat sandals, and the close-fitting leather leggings with their rows of elongated bone buttons, the short leather jacket and the big steeple-crowned sombrero of a *charro*. His fine, embroidered shirt was almost as dirty as Matt's, but silver gleamed in the concha on his chin string, in the inlay of his spurs and on the pommel and cantle of his saddle. The holster of his nickel-plated Colt was tied down.

The companion to whom he had spoken was a huge man, enormously fat, enormously dirty, glistening with sweat in his outsize *charro* rig. The bangs of his hair looked like a handful of black wire over his flat-planed, flat-nosed Indian face with its slanted eyes, jet in their folds of fat. His teeth were filed to points. Pure Yaqui, Matt thought.

Matt dismounted at the hitchrack and wrapped Pecas' rein around the rail.

At the sound of hoofbeats he turned. The slim Mexican stopped his roan six feet away and studied the spotted pony. The fat one led the gray around Matt and leaned his elbows on the hitchrack. The slender one spoke to him over Matt's head, as though Matt did not exist.

"Of truth, that is a horse! I, Chuy, say it! I will buy it from this stinking buffalo butcher."

He shifted his gaze to Matt. There was lazy insult in it. Matt ducked under the hitchrack so that he was no longer between the two.

The mounted *charro* said, "I will buy your 'orse. 'Ow much?"

"Not for sale," Matt said.

Through his clean white teeth, the Mexican said in Spanish, "May rats urinate on thy shriveled soul in thy stinking carcass!"

Matt answered in Spanish as though they were engaged in casual conversation, "It is presumed thou hast not been without soap and water for weeks as I have, yet thou hast the reek of broken wind from a vulture."

The *charro* grinned. "Thanks, friend! For the insult, I will kill thee! Lay the rifle down and step into the street. Draw the pistol when ready. I will wait."

From the tail of his eye Matt caught the sudden movement of loiterers stepping into doorways. A woman emerging from the store hastily dragged her child back inside. The small sounds of the plaza stopped.

Matt threw a hasty glance at the fat *charro*. He still leaned his elbows on the hitchrack, his opaque eyes avid.

The slender one said with exaggerated courtesy, "At your orders, Señor."

Matt's hand holding the Sharps began to sweat. "This is a matter for killing?" he asked.

"The insult was passed, Señor. It cannot be unsaid. I await your pleasure. Better that you step into the plaza, that the spectators have less risk."

Matt said, "I am not *pistolero*. I have no thirst for thy blood, nor to spill my own. I will commit suicide some other day."

He turned and walked steadily around the hitchrack. The muscles of his back cringed. He won't do it . . . not in the back . . . not with his pride, and people watching. . . .

The fat one dropped a thick hand onto the grip of his pistol. Matt started to swing the muzzle of the Sharps, but held the slight movement back.

He kept walking, stolidly, not looking back.

Behind him, the voice of the slender *charro* came loud, a speech for the onlookers who had gathered with the clairvoyance of buzzards: "Another *Yanqui*, Lázaro, with the strain of *mierda* on his back and a lack of tripes in his insides."

Lázaro said loudly, "I spit in the milk of his whore mother!"

Matt shouldered his way through a cluster of white men who grinned and Mexicans who did not, and stepped into the warm gloom of Daggett's saloon. As he walked to the bar, Frank Daggett stared at him without expression.

"Frank," Matt said, "gimme some of whatever poison you're sellin'. Have one yourself." He mopped his forehead with a sleeve.

Daggett looked at him with distaste but did not refuse the drink. It was several minutes before he recognized Matt. Then he grinned.

"Well now, by God, Matt! Where you been? Gonna stay around?"

"Well, maybe. Say Frank, what's chewin' the mane of that Mex'can? You see that ruckus?"

"Yeh, I seen it, Matt. It's happened before, same kind of a play."

"But what did he brace me for? First time I ever seen him that I know of!"

"Matt, Chuy Medina is poison! Don't fiddle with him, none at all! He's a real gun-hawk, I mean a real one! An' he hates all Americans. Any excuse is good enough for him, just so's they draw first. Long as he gives an even break, folks won't interfere. They're all scared to, anyway."

"But what the hell does he . . . he never even saw me before!"

"It ain't you, Matt, it's *any gringo*. He's downed two good men, gunfighters, men with reputations, an' a couple of others."

Daggett poured two drinks and glanced out through the window. "Matt, look," he said. "He's monkeyin' round that Injun horse of yours, right now!"

Matt set his drink on the bar and picked up the Sharps. He walked to the door and looked across the plaza. There, a hundred yards away, Chuy, the gunslinger, sat on his roan horse looking down at the spotted pony and talking to Lázaro. Lázaro picked up one of Pecas' hind hoofs.

"Get away from that horse!" Matt yelled in English.

"Eh?" Chuy cupped his hand behind his ear, assuming an expression of polite interrogation.

Matt snapped back the hammer of the Sharps.

"Now, Matt! Hey!" Daggett plucked at his sleeve.

Matt elbowed him away.

"Get away, Chuy!"

Matt braced the rifle against the door frame.

"But, Señor of the foul smell and the heart of a chicken, we but admire your little horse!" Chuy laughed.

Matt caught the big horn of Chuy's saddle on his front sight as though it were balanced there, and squeezed his hand shut. The recoil rocked him back. The saddle horn burst apart as though it had been a loaded bomb. The blast echoed back and forth across the plaza.

Chuy's roan reared and nearly went over backward. Lázaro sprinted for his mount.

As Matt reloaded and stepped into the street, Chuy

brought his horse under control and rode after the fat man.

Townspeople began to peek from doorways. A few stepped hesitantly into view. Running feet pounded. Matt watched the two *charros* ride out of sight around the last adobe at the end of the street.

A rough hand grabbed Matt's elbow and spun him around. The marshal with the long hair and the fancy gun belt glared into Matt's eyes.

"Gimme that Sharps! Nobody shoots no buffalo gun in my town!"

Matt jerked free. "Keep your hands off! Them Mex'cans is armed, both of 'em! Where were you?"

"I saw the whole thing," the marshal said. He reached for the rifle. Matt batted his hand away.

"You saw it, huh? You stood there an' watched that Mex tryin' to bait me into a killin'? You scared of him, with that Bill Hickok hair-do an' that six-gun? What are you, some kind of ornament?"

"Ornament! Why you goddamn gutless wonder! Let a lousy greaser back you down . . . take all them filthy words an' won't step out an' have it out with him!"

Matt was getting madder, if such a thing were possible. "I ain't no gun fighter!" he yelled.

"No, you sure ain't! But soon as you're out of pistol range, you're brave all right! Cut loose on him with that Sharps, a hundred yards away!"

"I ain't out of *your* range!" Matt shouted. He jammed the muzzle of the Sharps into the marshal's stomach and shoved him back against the rough adobe.

"*You're* wearin' that murderin' short gun! Go ahead, pull that Colt! *Pull* it!" He jammed the rifle harder into the marshal's belly. The marshal's hands went up as though jerked by strings.

"What the hell is this? I just ride in for a haircut an' a new shirt an' first thing I'm up to my ears in trouble!"

The marshal's face had a wooden look, but beads of sweat trickled down it.

"You keep out of my way!" Matt shouted into his face. "Lock yourself in your *cárcel! Vámos!*"

The marshal turned away, and Matt shoved him in the small of the back with the Sharps, making him take a few trotting steps.

Some of the townsmen were grinning. They looked at their feet or gazed into the sky when Matt's hot glance raked them.

Roughly, Matt shoved his way through the crowd to the Appaloosa.

Chapter 5

PECAS' hoofs were clattering across the loose planks of a small bridge over a dry *arroyo* before Matt remembered the haircut and the shirt and the other things he had not got in Ojo Prieto. Just ahead were the two tall poles and the high crossbar with the longhorn skull spiked to it, that marked the entrance to his own place. Fifty yards beyond, on top of a rise, four small black heads showed themselves against the sky.

"*Qué tal, chamacos?*" Matt called. "*Soy vuestro tío Mateo!*"

The heads ducked out of sight. Matt topped the rise in time to see three small figures scuttle under the brush *ramada* which shaded the door of his small adobe house. A toddler, female, naked and scared, squalled and ran after them. As she reached the door, three little heads, one above the other, peered from one side of the doorway. Around its other side Ana peered anxiously. In her arms was a naked infant, nursing sleepily.

Matt heeled Pecas into a trot and waved. Self-consciously, Ana pulled her blouse over her flat, exposed breast, and called, "Favor of returning later. My man is away."

Matt began to laugh.

"Do you not know your cousin, Anita? I am Mateo!"

He slid down, dropped the jaw rein and leaned the Sharps against a *ramada* post before turning to her.

"Mateo! Of truth? You are Mateo?"

"Of truth, under the beard and the dirt, I am Mateo!"

Her sudden smile was warm. She reached out both arms, then, her embarrassment obvious, offered one small hand in the abrupt, limp handshake of formality. Matt seized her waist and swung her in a great circle, kissed her loudly and set her down gently. Inside, the children squalled.

Paco Gómez rode in on a hammer-headed, vicious-eyed mule. He carried a hoe. He scowled to see the ragged, bearded stranger lying at ease in the hammock under the *ramada*. The stranger's indolent weight was augmented by that of four squirming children—Tomás, the eight-year-old, sat solemnly at the stranger's feet and gazed at the black-bearded face, hero-worship plain in his beautiful eyes. Raimundo, seven years, sat across the stranger's knees and played with a skinning knife which he had purloined from the quill-embroidered sheath on the stranger's belt. Paquita, who had four years (or was it five—who could remember these details?) bounced joyously on the stranger's flat stomach. Esmeralda, of two summers, and still nude, straddled the man's chest, greatly interfering with his efforts to drink from a *mezcal* jug. A *mezcal* jug! The jug of the nectar, the fiery *mezcal* from Bacanora! Holy Virgin of Guadalupe! Has Anita gone crazy?

Ana, her face alight with gaiety, came out with a bowl of fiery *chilis* and a plate of thin *tortillas*.

Grimly, Paco gripped the hoe and walked into view of the stranger, who set the jug on the ground behind a post. Then, with a yell, the bearded man erupted from the hammock, spilling small boys and girls onto the packed earth. Before Paco could swing the hoe, the stranger had seized him in a bear hug and swung him off the ground.

Suddenly Paco dropped the hoe and shouted, "Mateo! Mateo of my heart! It is you!"

Much later, when the shadow of the house stretched a hundred yards east across the *milpa* of stunted corn, Matt belched grandly and reached for the jug. He shook it anxiously. There was only a meager sloshing.

"There is another jug," Paco said. He sat slack-shouldered against a post. Ana emerged from the house with a last plate of thin *tortillas*.

"Woman, by the well, in a small hole under the flat rock . . ."

She set the plate down before Matt, looked accusingly at her husband, and walked to the well.

When she brought the jug, Matt said, "The jug, yes, Anita

de mi alma! But please, no more to eat! I have foundered myself!"

Paco pulled the plug and passed the jug to Matt. "Even while I was considering where to strike you with the hoe," he said, "with one eye I saw your horse. That is much horse!"

Matt groaned and got up. "I have watered him, but he should be fed again," he said. "Is there corn?" He was surprised to discover that his knees seemed to have no stiffening. That *mezcal* of Bacanora!

Tomás, the eight-year-old, said, "With permission, Uncle Mateo," and walked around behind the house.

"He will get the corn," Paco explained. "But is the horse safe for a child to approach? I see he is uncut, and although small, perhaps he—"

"Do not concern yourself, *'manito,'*" Matt assured him. "He is Indian. Small boys watch the pony herds and ride all day at a gallop, changing from horse to horse in mid-run. The stallion is accustomed to small horsemen. He is, of truth, strong and courageous, but never vicious."

"One would have to pay a fortune for such a horse," Paco said.

"I think I have bought him even more expensively," Matt said softly, and saw in his mind the spotted pony pounding away from Rath and Wright's soddy, with Wohk Pos Its already dead on its back and falling . . . and a picture clear as truth of Wo Ista, Buffalo Woman, with distorted, tear-wet face, holding up her left hand with one bloody stump where a slim brown finger had been. He reached for the jug and drank in great gulps until the liquor burned fire into his stomach. Paco shot one swift glance at him, then looked away.

Matt wiped his mouth. "What of the ranch, Paquito?" he asked briskly.

"The ranch," Paco said, "it is not good, but then—my apologies—it never was good."

"I know," Matt agreed. "It made no profit, even when my father ran it."

Paco went on, "One year there was a profit of eighty-five dollars. I saved it for you, but the next year there was sickness, and Ana lost the child, and I spent the money."

"No le hace!" Matt exclaimed. "Forget it! The ranch is as much yours as mine. Your mother and mine were cousins,

and you are as a brother. You are not my *peón*, to labor
and then hand over the profit of your work."

"Well, Mateo, there has been no profit, only that once.
But there are the goats for milk and most years, unless there
is drought, the corn and beans and *chilis* are sufficient. I
have the burro and the mule for plowing. The roof is tight,
the well water is good. What more shall a man ask? It is
a good life, and will be a good life for you, if you have
finished with wandering."

Matt said, "Perhaps soon it will be a better life for all. I
have an idea buzzing like a bee in my head. We will discuss
it at leisure."

Matt heard the rustle of corn-husk cigarette paper, and
soon caught the reek of rank tobacco. He said, "There was a
man in town today, a gunman. What of Chuy, a *charro*
who rides a roan horse?"

Paco drew on the cigarette. "You have seen Chuy? There
is a bad one. A youngster who was just a youngster until a
thing happened. Now he is an assassin, and chief of assassins."

"What thing happened, Paco?"

"It was nearly four years past. His family is the Medina.
Sometimes he gives himself the flattery of the full name,
Medina Mora—Jesús Medina Mora. The nickname, of course,
is 'Chuy.' At the time, he had fifteen years."

Paco pushed the *mezcal* jug within reach of Matt's hand.
Lazy and content, Matt listened.

"This Chuy was a novice in his father's business of *con-
trabandista*. All others in the enterprise were cousins, uncles,
brothers-in-law. You know this business, how it flourishes
out of the city of Chihuahua, and the valleys of the *sierra*?"

"Yes," Matt answered. "Big silver *pesos*, brought across the
river at night, avoiding the paying of export charges. Then
the purchase of goods on this side, anything scarce and
readily sold in Chihuahua or Sonora at a miser's profit. It
is a long-established business. Why should it make an assassin of Chuy?"

"There is more background." Paco was not to be hurried.
"The Medina, little by little, discouraged rivalry. They traveled in strength, with a rifleman for every three burros in
the pack train. Their strong defense discouraged those who
would have ambushed them, and there were few attempts to
raid their trains."

"What of authority?" Matt asked. "Has there been no law enforcement?"

Paco smiled grimly. "Authority? There is none, except what little the Rangers exert here and in Texas, and a few of the military in Mexico. No, even before the war, it was very bad—now the border for hundreds of miles is only cattle thievery and horse stealing and good people murdered in bed."

"Revolution was in the air," Paco went on, "and there were guerrillas looting and raping in the name of Liberty, and those in office were venal, and Medina bribery was liberal. Their competition faded away, of a *maguey* rope with a noose, or a .44 slug in the head. The Medina ran their burro trains almost on a schedule, like the stage from Chihuahua to El Paso del Norte."

"You are a long time getting to Chuy," Matt complained. "He was ready to kill me today, and I was scared."

Paco's startled eyes gleamed pale in the glow of his cigarette. "You looked down his gun? And you are here to tell it? You must tell me!" But he was not to be diverted. "A man came to Ojo Prieto, and he was *pistolero*, a bad man. He swaggered in Daggett's saloon and got drunk and made a big noise, but it was plain that he was dangerous, and no one opposed him. The Medina silver trains were common knowledge. After several weeks, this curly-haired swaggering *gringo* went away.

"Then, a month later, Chuy Medina Mora, the youth, came with a burro train out of Chihuahua. The trip was made boldly in daylight, and the Medina rode carelessly. There were nineteen of them, and forty burros, heavy laden. In that little *arroyo*, you know? That deep one that leads to the ford? There, the guns opened fire. Along both sides of the *barranca*.

"The burros pitched and rolled with their loads and scattered up and down the *arroyo*. And the careless Medina died. To a man, they died, some with their carbines still in the saddle boots, some in a circle of spent cartridges, behind dead horses or spilled packs of silver coins. All but Chuy.

"And there, we of the town and the nearby ranches found them, led to them by the far sound of gunfire and the vultures. Two dead *gringos* were found also, men of the stamp of the curly-haired swaggerer—and signs of seven others, and the tracks of eight burros driven away with their loads. We found Chuy, lying with his broken leg pinned under his mount. But the curly-haired one we did not find. That one died only three months ago, in Tres Piedras, in the street.

"It is said that someone brought word to Chuy that this curly-head was in Tres Piedras. Chuy went there and taunted him in the street and killed him. It was fair. The *gringo* tried for his gun, but it never cleared the holster. Chuy spat on his body, asked if there was some other *gringo* present who wished to cut a notch in his gun handle for a dead 'greaser,' and when none accepted, rode away.

"Chuy is fast with a gun. Very fast. He is touched in the head, perhaps, by the tragedy of his dead father, his three brothers, and various uncles and cousins in that *arroyo*."

"He is a rabid coyote," Matt said. "He had never seen me before, but he wanted to kill me. Why me? Would he think that I was at that *arroyo*?"

"No, Mateo. Any *gringo* who wears a gun is his victim. Three have died in Ojo Prieto, contemptuous of a Mexican gunman. Others have died in other towns. It is Chuy's pride to cut them down with their own chosen weapon."

"But Paco," Matt objected, "it is true that Mexicans do not match the *gringo* gunfighters with the handgun. How did Chuy acquire the skill?"

"How is it true, Mateo? There is still the hand, the eye, the nerve and the practice. The Colt .44 makes no distinction in the color of the hand that masters it. You were lucky! What occurred?"

"I was scared, Paco! I suffered bitter shame, but I walked away alive. Well, I will keep out of his way. Now, tell of this marshal, this boor with the loud mouth and the fancy gun. He thought that, since I had balked at Chuy, I would balk at him, but I rearranged his thoughts. What eats at his pride?"

"Well, Mateo, make no mistake, he too is a dangerous man! But Chuy is deadlier. He ordered Chuy to leave his gun in Daggett's saloon while he was in town, and Chuy laughed at him and invited him to take the gun. The marshal backed down, and ever since he thinks to regain his pride by bullying lesser men.

"But Chuy cannot last, Mateo. He does not confine himself to smuggling, now. His arrogance grows with each killing. He has gathered bravos and cut-throats, Yaquis and renegades. Now, they dare to rob the mail coaches. *Gringo*

prospectors are murdered in the *sierra*. Even his own people, the ox-drivers, the farmers, the harmless small people
suffer his greed. He has taken over a small town, Cocatlán,
in the shadow of the Sierra Madre, where he and his bravos
live like generals, taking what pleases them of women, horses,
anything that strikes their fancy. He will digest a knife in his
tripes one fine night!"

Matt was suddenly surfeited with the gloomy talk. "Paco,"
he said, "let us forget this murdering Chuy. I will avoid him.
Let us have one more drink, and save some *mezcal* for tomorrow. It is good to be with my own people!"

The *mezcal* jug rose and gurgled, first above Matt's tilted
head, then over Paco's.

"Good night, brother!"

"Sleep well, brother!"

Paco stepped into the house and Matt went to the hammock.

Chapter 6

PACO LOUNGED against the door frame. The first sunlight,
slanting in under the *ramada*, touched the flat contours of his
brown face and burnished the blue highlights on the straight
black hair, cut in a bang, Comanche fashion, across his
forehead. Ana knelt before the *metate*, rocking back and
forth in a rhythm as old as time, rubbing the *mano* up and
down the groove in the lava rock, grinding the corn into
coarse flour.

Four small Gómez—Tomás, Raimundo, Paquita, and
Esmeralda—stood watching Matt strop the skinning knife
on the side of his boot. The baby lay contented beside his
mother.

Matt seized a fistful of beard and hacked it off close to his
chin. Ana stopped her grinding to watch. Esmeralda, like a
small, fat nymph, moved closer. Raimundo gazed in open-
mouthed fascination. Matt sawed away and the gouts of
whiskers fell about his feet until his face was covered only
by a pelt like the close-curled wool of a burro colt.

"Favor of hot water, Tomás," Matt said, "and is there soap?"

Tomás brought a bowl of hot water from the *brasero* and a dish of harsh soap, an emulsion of boiled fat and wood ashes. Matt rubbed soap and water into the stubble and made the first careful shaving stroke down his outraged cheek.

"Ow! Goddamn! I'd rather be scalped!"

"Goddamn," said Esmeralda, solemnly.

When the last stiff black whisker was scraped away, Ana said, laughing, "You look like—I do not know what! With the face brown like any good Mexican's, only the chin white as a *gringo's* where it is not red and lacerated. Now sit still, lest you lose an ear, and I will attack the buffalo mane on the rest of your head."

Later, with the children driven away and Ana discreetly keeping to the house, Matt peeled off his smelly clothes and hung them on the well sweep. He soaped his hard body, then stood shivering while Paco poured bucket after bucket of water over him.

Paco remarked, "On your back, under the shoulder blade, is that a *cornada*? It appears like the wound of a *matador*, except that it is not in the belly or thigh. You must have been running!" He grinned, and touched the scar.

"Yes, it is a horn thrust, from a buffalo cow that should have been dead but was not. My life was saved by my friend Karl Koch."

"Ah-h-h! Karl Koch!" Paco nodded. "He has the fame of marksmanship, even in these parts. It is said none can match him."

"Well, Paco, forgive the immodesty, but I will match him at any distance, with the big Sharps. And at a moving target, I will beat him."

Matt reached for his foul shirt and began to dry himself with it. "Whew! This stinks! I cannot wear it again. I shall have to go naked, like Esmeralda. But now, while we are alone, and your children are not swarming over me like cowbirds on a buffalo, let us discuss that idea of mine."

"*Bueno*, brother, but first—you are indecent!" Paco said, and roared at the house, "Tomás!"

Tomás' head popped around the corner.

"Bring a clean *camisa* and *calzones* for your uncle! And the jug of *mezcal*!"

Tomás brought the jug and the clean white shirt and the

cotton pants which looked like tapering underdrawers. With a feeling of luxury, Matt pulled the shirt over his shorn head and hauled up the *calzones,* tying the tabs in front of his stomach.

Paco said, "Now go somewhere, Tomás, your uncle and I have a thing to discuss."

Matt sat on the well curb and pulled the boy onto his lap. "No, let him stay. This is not a secret thing." Then, "A moment, Tomás. Is the spotted horse watered and fed?"

"Before the sun rose," the boy answered.

"Thanks, *chamaco!* Now, Paco," Matt settled himself comfortably, "we discuss this horse. How is he, in your opinion?"

"*Bién,* Mateo, since you ask—I know nothing of his obedience and endurance, except what you have said. But I like better a bigger mount. The *gringos* cross hot-blooded stock with the mustang strain, and get horses of sixteen hands even, with intelligence and toughness. Your *macho* is small, like the cow ponies of the Texas brush country. Nevertheless —and this is not to flatter you—for his size, I have never seen a horse equal to your Pecas. I went to greet him this morning and he came to me like a child's pet, and I studied him with eye and hand. There is no fault, not one, nothing! He is a mount for a hero! Whence comes this strain of spotted horse?"

Matt took a drink from the jug and wiped his mouth, which felt strange in its lack of whiskers.

"They say," he said, "that many years ago, a Jesuit *padre* went as missionary to the Nez Percé. They had horses of this spotted strain, but they were just *mesteños* like those of other Indians. This *padre* was rider almost to equal the Comanche. He knew blood lines and breeding. He taught the Nez Percé the art of castration and helped them to select the best studs and brood mares. Now, after a century, they have the best horse-flesh in all America, and a sound Appaloosa is worth thirty Indian ponies. A fine one is the most valued possession of any Plains warrior, and is buffalo runner and war horse, never used for other work."

"This is most interesting," Paco said. "I am glad for you." He pushed away from the well sweep on which he had been leaning. "Now, I must get at that upper *milpa.* You have the appetite of a bitch wolf with nine pups; therefore, I must grow much corn."

"Wait," Matt said. He rose and set Tomás down. "Tomás, will you leave us now, please? Ride the stallion a while to exercise him. Perhaps for an hour, then stake him in a fresh place."

"Thank you, Tió Mateo!" The boy's pleasure showed in his black eyes. He turned and ran.

Matt pushed aside the greasy pants on the well sweep and picked up the buckskin moneybelt which was underneath. He handed it to Paco.

Paco looked at him questioningly, felt the heft of it in his hand, then unfastened the lacing of one flap. Many gold double-eagles were inside. He pursed his lips in a silent whistle. "You are wealthy, Mateo," he said.

"*We* are wealthy, to a small degree, '*manito*," Matt corrected. "This money will work for us. First we must fence part of the ranch."

"Fencing? For what?" Paco inquired. "I keep the devil mule hobbled, and it seems your stallion is no runaway."

"Fencing for the wives of the stallion, the brood mares, and many fine, spotted Appaloosa colts," Matt explained, grinning widely.

"Eh?" Paco's eyes widened.

"Pecas will be the perfect stud!" Matt exclaimed. "We start with half a dozen brood mares, perhaps of Kentucky stock, to give size. Every plainsman knows the endurance, the easy-keeping of the Appaloosa. Ranchers will want them —the Comancheros will buy, for trade with the Comanche. Comanches themselves will buy, and pay with the rich loot from Mexico. *We* will be wealthy, Paco! You are my full partner!"

Paco embraced him, hugging hard. "I thank you, brother! Let us go and study the best place for pasture and feed racks. I will get a *reata*, and we will measure for fencing." His grin was ecstatic.

"Throw that hoe away, Paco! We will *buy* corn!"

A mile from the house, where the corner of the property was marked with a cairn of rocks, Matt squatted holding the honda of the *reata* over a mark scratched on the ground. Paco tugged the *reata* tight and marked under its end with his toe.

"Another ten *varas*," he called. "How many does that make?"

Matt scratched "10" with a nail on the board which held the record. "Let's see," he said, "85, 95, 105. A hundred and fifteen *varas*, and we are about half way around." He squatted on his bare heels. "This will make a fine pasture for the mares and the little *potros*. For the yearlings, we will fence that swale that has the good grass."

Suddenly he stood up. "A horseman comes!" he warned. "I feel it in the ground."

Paco stood hastily and shaded his eyes, peering in the direction of the house which was hidden by a swell of ground.

"Goddamn it!" Matt exploded in English, "Goddamn me for a fool! I left the Sharps under the *ramada*!"

"Wait, Mateo, do not excite yourself. It is only a burro. I hear the choppy trot. Probably Tomás has found the jug and understood our need." Paco paused. "One thought, though . . ." Worry creases ridged his forehead. "That burro will not run, even under threat of a stick. There must be urgency, if Tomás has succeeded in making him run!"

Tomás came into view. The burro slowed to a sulky walk. The boy cut it across the ears with a quirt, cruelly, and it went into a jarring lope. Suddenly Paco ran to meet his son.

"Mateo, come! There is trouble!" he yelled over his shoulder. "Tomás is crying! He never cries!"

Paco swept Tomás from the burro's back and held him close. The boy's face was distorted and streaked with tears. His shirt was torn and the small brown shoulder showed scraped and bleeding. He was saying something, but the speech was so garbled by sobs that it could not be understood.

Paco shook him gently and smoothed back his tousled hair. The boy stopped sobbing and gazed into his father's eyes while tears spilled over and ran down past his nose.

"The stallion!" he blurted. "The stallion!"

Matt threw down the tally board and began to run. He skidded to a stop and ran back to snatch up the *reata*. Paco was already running, carrying the boy. When Matt overtook them, Paco said to Tomás, "Now, tell!"

Matt jogged alongside, impatient at Paco's slower pace. Jerkily, Tomás said, "They took him—drove him off!"

"Who? Who did this?" Paco demanded.

"Two *charros* . . . a fat one . . . a thin one! I was

riding Pecas and they came over the hill . . . galloping
. . . They swung *reatas!*"

Paco cursed.

"I slapped Pecas . . . he ran . . . the thin man roped
me and I fell. The other . . . on the gray horse . . . he
roped the stallion. I could not see it all. I was . . . on the
ground."

"Stop crying, son, and tell!" Paco grunted. "It was not
your fault!"

"I got the rope off . . . my mother came running . . .
she had . . . the hoe . . . the thin one rode at her, he
tried to . . . ride her down, she dodged and, and—" Tomás'
sobbing broke forth afresh.

"Now son," Paco insisted, "you must tell quickly!"

"She dodged away, *papá* . . . and as he passed, he . . .
struck with the quirt. The man . . . rode back to the stallion
and quirted the stallion and . . . he quirting and the fat
one pulling, they . . . rode fast . . . over the hill."

"And your mother?"

"She is all right, papá. But her face pains where . . .
the *romal* whipped her . . . she got your quirt and we . . .
caught the burro and . . . she said, 'Make him run!' She
said to . . . bring you and Tió Mateo!"

"You go ahead, Mateo," Paco grunted. "I will not leave
the child but I will come fast!"

Matt cursed his bare feet and the stubble that punctured
them and the stones that bruised them, but would not defer
to them. He ran heedless and reckless, and refused to slow
down until he reached the *ramada* and got down the buffalo
gun. He groped in the roof thatch for the bag of shells.

Ana sat in the hammock with her frightened children huddled around her. Her left eye was swollen shut, and there
was a livid blue streak running from her temple down across
her face, and blood on her lips where the lash had cut.

Matt opened the breech of the Sharps enough to see the
cartridge in the chamber. He tried to put shells in a pants
pocket, but there was no pocket in the *calzones,* so he slung
the bag over his shoulder by its drawstring.

As soon as he began to run, he began to think he wouldn't
make it on his lacerated feet, but he ground his teeth together and kept on as hard as he could go, to the top of the
rise overlooking the bridge. As he ran, Paco shouted after

him, "Mateo, it is useless! They are far away by now!" But Matt paid no attention, just kept running.

And at the top of the hill, there was nothing to see except the marks where a horse had slid going down. There was not even dust rising, just the road wandering away toward the Río Grande and disappearing in the *chaparral*. He limped back to the house.

Paco and Ana and the children watched in silence.

He leaned against the adobe and said, "Ana, favor of bringing my boots."

Ana said, "But, Mateo, they are broken! The sole on the left—"

"Get them!" he roared, and she bowed her head and went inside.

Paco said, "There is no need to speak to the woman that way."

"Shut your mouth! And get the mule!"

"Mateo, show sense! It is useless! You cannot—"

"Will you, Paco, or must I? Is there a saddle?"

"In the second room," Paco answered brusquely. "You are fool!" He caught up the *reata* from where Matt had flung it down, and walked away.

Ana brought the boots and dropped them on the ground. "Your boots," she said, and went back into the house. Matt stared after her for a moment, then shrugged and picked up a boot.

His swollen foot would go into the boot top, but not past the heel. He swore and threw the boot as far as he could and limped into the house.

"Ana, I need bandage and grease."

She went into the back room and, in a few moments, flung out a ragged *camisa*. "There is soap. No grease," she said tonelessly.

"And the saddle, will you bring it?" he asked, and tore the shirt into strips and went out to the hammock and began to bandage his feet.

Ana came out with the saddle, set it on the ground at his feet and went back inside. He remembered this Mexican saddle that had been his father's, its tight white rawhide cover dusty, the rigging exposed and fastened around the fork at the base of the big dinner-plate horn, the big *tapaderos* shaped like wooden Dutch shoes.

There was a trampling and snorting behind the house, and

Paco came dragging the rawboned mule, with its head high and its eyes rolling white.

Paco stood watching as Matt tried to secure the bandages. At length he said, "This mule will give you nothing but trouble."

Matt was a little shocked by Paco's use of the formal *"usted"* rather than the brotherly *"tu."* He's sore, he thought. Well, I'm sorry, but . . .

"If there are spurs, I will ride him," he said. "And I will feed *him* trouble with the quirt until it runs out his ears!"

"There are spurs," Paco said, but he made no move to get them. "Brother," he said, and now he used the friendly *'tu,'* "are you then so determined about this horse?"

"I will get him back. And nothing will stop me—not Chuy, not Lázaro, and not you."

Paco kicked dirt. "I owe Chuy for the roping of Tomás," he said, "and for the mark on Ana's face. But I will not charge bellowing after them like a bull with a prickly pear up his *culo.* I will not forget, but I will wait. But do not forget, Mateo, a retaliation against Chuy is not against him alone, but also against Lázaro and many other murdering *hideputas.* One must go carefully."

"Go *you* carefully, Paco," Matt said shortly. "I go after my horse."

He rose, picked up the saddle, and started toward the mule.

Paco sighed. He said, "Go then, fool."

"You said that before, Paco. Do not say it again."

Then Matt put the saddle down and laid his hand on Paco's shoulder. "I *am* fool, Paco, to quarrel with you. I will not leave you in anger. Can you not see—to you, a horse is a horse, however fine, and not worth risk, or even much trouble. This Pecas, to me, he is—many things I cannot explain. Chuy made me crawl once. I would not deliberately seek him out merely for the revenge of insult. But to that humiliation he has added the theft of Pecas, and I do not accept."

Paco turned and smiled at him. "This I understand, Mateo. I know you well, and if you must, you must. But, first, the mule is too slow to catch him. So you would ride into his country on a mule that will bedevil you all the way. You will meet his spy in every oxdriver and *cantinero,* with your great gun which says, 'See, I am *gringo* buffalo hunter!' You might as well have a target on your back and a sign saying, 'Shoot and collect the blood money from Chuy.' He will expect pursuit at once. A week from now, he will think you have abandoned it. Let us take time to plan and prepare. Perhaps we can think him to death."

Matt said, "You have reason, brother. I knew I was wrong. So tonight we talk, but—I will have my horse back!"

Chapter 7

THE SMALL children were abed. Ana lay back in the hammock silent, listening as her husband and her cousin-by-marriage began to make the plan. Pale stars had begun to show, Matt shifted his back restlessly against the *ramada* post. The hard-packed earth gave back the heat of the day along the length of his stretched-out legs.

"There is no more need to argue, Paco, I will go as a Mexican—some footloose *vaquero* or small *ranchero*, just a casual traveler, perhaps looking for old-time friends or relatives, or as one fleeing the Rangers. I must have a horse, if you will find one for me, and I will wear the Mexican clothing my father left."

"Well, Mateo, your speech is authentic, and it is fortunate that your father had the conceit of playing *charro*—the clothing is suitable. And your appearance is not *gringo*, except the green eyes, and they do not signify, really. There is much Anglo blood in Chihuahua, even blue eyes and freckles. How soon will you need the horse?"

"Right away. Tomorrow. I will go warily, but I will lose no time."

"But Mateo! Tomorrow! I cannot find a good horse tomorrow! It takes time! Horse buying is a matter of calculated insult and scoffing and haggling."

"Paco, get me a horse tomorrow. The sorrier the better, in keeping with this slovenly *vaquero* who will be Matt Fletcher. These damned feet won't let me travel for a day or so, but I will have time to get acquainted with the horse."

Paco gave up. "Let us look at the clothing, Ana." Ana went inside. Matt heard her light the lantern, then the creak of old leather as she opened the trunk in the back room. She returned presently with an armful of clothing.

Paco spread out the long, wrinkled *charro* leggings with their rows of bone buttons down the sides, and a short leather jacket with faded embroidery of the eagle-snake-cactus emblem on its back, and a wide-brimmed straw sombrero from Jalisco. Flat-heeled sandals and a pair of spurs with six cruel points on each big rowel completed the costume.

"These will fit you reasonably well. It is certain they will not be too small. All is authentic for your part as small rancher. There is also your father's old Henry rifle and a scabbard for it."

"The scabbard will not hold the Sharps," Matt objected. "I will carry it across my arm, as always."

"You will not carry the Sharps! You must be *ranchero* in every detail and action. The Henry rifle is appropriate. The Sharps is not. And I still say you are fool to go at all, because I am afraid for you."

"Well, I suppose you are right about the big rifle," Matt conceded. "Are there loads for the Henry?"

"No. Only three shells. Tomorrow I go to Ojo Prieto for cartridges."

"That is why I do not like the Henry," Matt complained, "and those rimfire shells that cannot be reloaded."

"Mateo, you must not leave for several days," Paco insisted. "Make up your mind to it. First, there are the cartridges, and there will be other things you will need. Oil and saddle soap, so your gear will look well-used. Ana must have time to fix the clothing. Your feet must heal a little more, and you should get plenty of sun on your shaven chin. Let the beard grow to cover it. Three or four days of beard is in character."

"Does this *ranchero* carry his pistol?" Matt asked sarcastically, "or do you deprive me of that, also?"

"By all means, the pistol!" Paco laughed. "It is old and worn, exactly suitable for our down-at-heels *ranchero*."

Matt got the old cap-and-ball revolver from his war bag, a Whitney Navy Colt, model 1861. He checked the .36 caliber loads in its six chambers and replaced the percussion caps, and let the hammer down between two nipples for safety. As an afterthought, he withdrew the assembly of rammer

lever and cylinder pin, and removed the loaded cylinder.
He put the spare cylinder in place and reassembled the revolver. Carefully, he poured black powder from the flask
into each chamber, rammed home the greased pistol balls.
He took the primer caps from the loose cylinder and put
them on the one in the pistol.

He said, "As you see, Paco, I take your advice. I over-
look no little detail, even to an extra loaded cylinder for
the pistol. I will carry it in my pocket, in case I must shoot
twelve assassins in a hurry, instead of only six—that is,
after I have fired the sixteen loads from the Henry rifle."

"You make fun of me, Mateo," Paco smiled. "But, who
knows, you may need every shot at your command. But
you removed the caps from the nipples!"

"A precaution," Matt explained. "If one falls on a rock, or
is kicked by a horse, all six loads may blast one's buttocks
off if the loads are primed. Is there beeswax, perhaps,
and a small wad of cotton?"

"Yes," Ana said. "With my needles and thread, Paco, in
the small basket."

When Paco brought the lump of wax and the cotton,
Matt put the wax into a tin cup and balanced it on the lantern. While the wax was melting, he wrapped six percussion caps in cotton and inserted the wad into the center pin-
hole of the cylinder. Carefully he dipped the loaded cylinder
into the cup and rolled it until it had a smooth, thin coating
of wax. "Perhaps my new horse will toss me into the river,"
he said. "At least, I will have six dry loads."

Matt fretted through the next day, lying in the hammock
and bathing his swollen feet, while Ana worked on the
clothing. She refastened the cylindrical bone buttons on the
leggings and cut the bottoms shorter, shortened the sleeves
of the jacket and polished the silver coins which served as
sleeve buttons. She brushed the *sombrero* with a handful of
stiff yucca leaves. It was still battered, and the brim was
badly frayed. All day, she scarcely spoke. Her silence
and the corresponding solemnity of the children finally got
on Matt's nerves, and he said, "What is the matter with you,
Ana? Are you still angry for my harsh words yesterday?
I apologized. You might make allowances because I was up-
set over the horse."

She looked at him and her eyes brimmed with tears. "I
am afraid for you, Mateo. I cannot be gay."

Ashamed, he patted her shoulder. "Sister, do not be foolish. I am careful. I am the most cautious of men. Nothing will happen to me."

In late afternoon, Paco rode in on the mule, leading a gaunted bay horse with a blazed face. Not a spirited mount, by its looks, but not badly put up. If there were only time to feed it up a little, perhaps grain for a couple of weeks . . .

Paco tossed a box of .44 rimfire cartridges to Matt and dismounted. "These are old, Mateo. McAleer found them on a back shelf. I hope they are still good."

"Thanks, Paco. What of the horse? You know him?" Matt reached for the halter, and the bay shied wildly and jerked at the lead rope.

"Head-shy," Matt grunted in exasperation. "Someone has beat him. Saddle-galled, too! Is this the best. . . ?"

Paco was leading the mule away to hobble it. He stopped and called over his shoulder, "You said to bring a horse today, Mateo. If I could have looked farther, or bargained to better advantage, but old Blás sensed my haste. I had to pay eighteen dollars, too. At any rate, he is rope-broke."

Moving slowly and talking quietly, Matt managed to lead the bay to a stake where Pecas had been tied. It promptly tangled its forefeet in the picket rope, and, when Matt approached to free it, lurched away and fell heavily. Matt risked a kick in the head and got it untangled and led it to the *ramada*, where he tied it short so it could not get a foot over the rope.

Paco had brought a small can of axle grease. That evening Matt wrapped his feet in greased bandages and tried on the *guaraches*, the flat sandals that had been his father's. Later, he took the Henry rifle and reflected light into its breech with a piece of paper, and was gratified to see that there was only slight pitting, way back by the chamber. Paco had cared for it well. He loaded the tubular magazine, pulling back the spring and anchoring it at the muzzle end and sliding the full load of fifteen cartridges one by one into the slot. He worked the lever rapidly, and the ejector picked the shells out neatly and flipped them over his shoulder. Satisfied, he reloaded the magazine and put the rifle into the freshly oiled saddle scabbard.

Just before he climbed into the hammock, he said to Paco, "I will not be gone long, if the bay horse is any good. I will estimate two weeks, three at the most. I will take a

hundred dollars. It is better that you keep the rest. When I
come back, we will start buying mares."

"Well, then." Paco took the coins. "I will wrap them in
cloth and put them in a tin can and hide them in the hole
under the rock. There by the well sweep, where I had the
mezcal jug. When do you leave?"

"At daylight tomorrow."

"Mateo, your feet are still lame. You have not tried out the
bay. Will you not—no, I see you will not. Ana has made
pinole for you, and there is meat wrapped in *tortillas* for
the first day."

Matt slept lightly and woke before daylight. He winced at
his sore feet when he got down from the hammock, and left
the bandages on as he tied on the *guaraches*. A movement
in the doorway caught his attention, and he turned to see
Ana silently hugging herself in the dawn chill.

"You are up early, sister," Matt said.

"I could not sleep. I have been praying."

While he breakfasted, Paco brought in the blaze-faced
bay, saddled it and packed the saddlebags and hung an old
army canteen on the horn. The bay's bridle, also an in-
heritance from Matt's father, was a simple headstall. The
vicious spade bit had heavy cheeks decorated with silver
inlay.

Matt arose from his flat-heeled squat and handed his empty
plate to Ana. "Thank you, sister," he said, and felt the
pockets of the jacket to be sure that one held the spare
cylinder for the pistol, and the other sixteen rimfire .44s,
a spare load for the rifle. He felt behind his right hip, to
make sure the skinning knife was firm in its quilled and
fringed Cheyenne sheath.

One by one, he picked up the five children and kissed
them. He shook hands with Tomás, as man to man. Ana
embraced him and laid her cheek against his. He kissed her
gently, tasting the salt of tears.

"Anita," he said, and laughed softly, "this is not the Day
of the Dead. I but go to recover a stolen horse. It has been
done many times."

"Go with God, Mateo! The Blessed Virgin watch over
thee!"

Matt patted her shoulder and turned to see Paco emerging
from the house with a *serape*. Matt recognized the brilliant
stripes of the Saltillo style, so close-woven it would turn rain.

"Take it," Paco said. "Nights can be cold in the *sierra*."

Matt tied the *serape* behind the cantle of the saddle. Paco embraced him, cheek to cheek, first one side and then the other. "You remember the way to Cocatlán, as I told you? Just follow the main *carretera*."

The bay slung its head when Matt reached for the braided reins. He turned it in a half circle and swung up into the saddle.

Paco reached and caught a bit chain. "Mateo," he said, "do this for me and for Ana, who love you—go warily, every minute, lest you end in some dry *barranca* as meat for buzzards. I think you do not understand how Chuy dominates around Cocatlán, and even all the way from the river. Every *campesino* and *vaquero* may be his spy, through fear. Every stranger arouses suspicion. It is like a world of wild beasts. Trust no one, *no one!* Be alert, even when you sleep. And if any little thing does not seem right, give up the horse and come back. Even if you think I am an old woman with the guts of a chicken, trust my judgment in this. You have been away—you do not know how things are."

Matt ruffled Paco's black hair. "I will remember, *'manito.*" He tightened the rein slightly, remembering the spade bit, touched the bay lightly with one spur, and it went into a trot.

Chapter 8

MATT FOLLOWED the narrow two-wheel track of the *carretera* between crowding, chest-high borders of *chaparral*. The wind rattled the drying pods thrusting up from the clustered daggers of soapweed and made the bay nervous. Matt had to watch the horse's twitching ears and talk it out of bolting each time they passed a dark mesquite with its lacy branches whipping.

He had hoped for an easy fording of the river, but the thirty yards of dark, slow water scared the bay again, and he had to wrench the blaze-faced head around with a harsh pull on the spade bit. Finally, under the spurs, it grunted and went into the water with a great plunging leap. For a few yards in the middle, it lost footing and Matt rode hunched, ready to slide off. The horse found bottom again and surged out, shying at tule reeds on the Mexican bank. Then it wanted to run, and Matt let it go until it had run itself out. When it began to blow and wanted to slow to a walk, he made it trot, for discipline and to prevent chilling.

The country opened out and the wind had a clear sweep at them. The flying dust turned to mud in the wrinkles of Matt's wet leggings, and he could taste it, bitter and gritty on his teeth.

In mid-morning, a burro train showed far ahead, coming north. For a bad moment, with Chuy and his smuggling trains in mind, Matt looked for cover and found none, and eased the rifle out of its scabbard under his right leg. He levered a cartridge into the chamber and lowered the hammer to half-cock, but put the rifle back when he made out the straggly loads of firewood on the half dozen burros and saw that there were only two riders, also on burros.

A half hour later, when they passed, he grinned and said, *"Qué hubo?"* but the two men hurried their animals past and would not look at him.

Late in the afternoon the wind increased and, as the slanting sunlight began to lose authority, cold crept in under the tail of the short jacket and through the thin *camisa*. Far ahead, alone in a flat expanse of brown earth, stood a building, stark and bare. There was a gallery-like cloister across its front, behind graceful crumbling arches.

Matt whacked the bay with the *romal* braided into the end of the reins, and it broke grudgingly into a canter. Fifty yards from the building, a wind-hounded tumbleweed came rolling from behind and swept past.

The bay horse blew up.

Taken by surprise, Matt lost a stirrup, but managed to hook a spur under the saddle skirt and ride the flurry out. The bay was not ready to quit, but had not the heart to fight the spade bit when Matt yanked its head up and pulled it to a plunging halt. He dismounted and led it to a hitch-rack in front of the building, where two skinny saddled horses stood shifting nervously. Scaling painted letters on a gallery column said, "Posada del León."

A tousle-headed, unshaven man wearing an apron watched from the doorway as Matt tied the bay.

"A cold day for a long ride, *amigo*," Matt said, "but the last ten *varas* were warm enough, when that stupid horse broke in two! Your inn is timely for a cold and hungry man."

The man stared and did not answer, but stood stolidly with the door half open behind him. Matt walked across the gallery on the broken red tiles, and paused, waiting for the man to let him pass inside. Over the man's shoulder he could see two *vaqueros* at a table, with a bottle between them.

Matt said, "I wish corn for my horse, and water, as a favor. And *tequila* for myself, first, before I consider dinner."

The man did not move. He said, "There is nothing."

"Eh?" Matt's grin faded. "I see the sign, 'Posada.' Is this not an inn?"

"The accommodations are full," the man said.

Matt thought about this for a moment, then turned away. He stopped and swung back. "At least, water for the horse," he said.

"No."

Matt walked back to the hitchrack and untied the bay. It was too tired to shy. He mounted and sat for a moment with his hands resting on the horn, looking at the man in the doorway. The two *vaqueros* came up behind the man and stood staring over his shoulder at Matt.

"Is there a place where I may stay the night—some village or *poblado* which I will reach before dark?" he asked.

No one answered.

Matt reined the bay around and urged it into a trot.

A little before dusk, he found a shallow *arroyo* that carried no water, but supported brush on its banks and a few straggly cottonwoods and willows. He followed it half a mile from the road, then went down a dim game trail through the brush to the bottom.

In the creek bed, he scooped a hollow in the sand and found dampness. Twenty minutes of hand digging made a basin the size of a wash tub into which slow water began to seep. While he waited for it to collect, he put a hobble on the horse, tying the *mecate* loosely above the front fetlocks in the hope that the weary animal would graze on the scanty grass among the clumps of wickedly-thorned *tornillo*. The bay immediately began to jump with its bound forefeet and trot with the hind ones, moving so rapidly that Matt had to run to catch it. He tied it to a tree and brought cottonwood branches to eke out the sparse grass. There was now a hatful of bitter, alkaline water in the hole. Matt filled his tin cup and made a meal of *tortillas* and goat meat. Then he led the bay to the hole, where enough water had gathered for one long drink. He tied the horse again, rolled up in the *serape* and went to sleep.

The crazy squalling of coyotes woke him in the false dawn. He rose, stiff and cramped, and untangled the bay's feet from the *mecate*. There were two or three gallons of water in the hole and enough light to show his reflection. Whiskers and the chopped-off hair gave him a tough look.

Well, I look enough like any ragged-ass *vaquero* now. Nobody would take me for the scared buffalo hunter that backed down from Chuy at Ojo Prieto.

He filled the canteen, then got *pinole* from the saddle bag and stirred it in the cup with water, and drank down the mixture of parched corn flour and dark sugar. The bay flung up its head in a half-hearted way when he untied the *mecate* from the tree, but followed him eagerly to the water and drank. It accepted the bit when Matt poked his thumb into the back of its mouth, then humped its back against the cold of the saddle blanket. Matt was reaching to pick up the saddle when he heard the sound of hoofs, walking, up on the bank behind thick brush.

Matt glanced at his pistol which lay ten feet away on the *serape* where he had slept. Then he cautiously slipped his left arm through the reins and drew the Henry rifle from the saddle scabbard. He remembered that he had loaded the chamber when he had seen the burro drivers the day before. He squatted a moment, listening, then took a turn with the reins around the saddle horn to anchor the horse, and stepped softly four paces to one side and lay full length behind a clump of *huisache*.

He heard the creak of saddle leather, the sound a stirrup leather might make while a man dismounted.

The brush moved, and a man came down the slope. Only his head and shoulders showed above the brush, and, behind him, the head of the horse he was leading. Matt's bay horse whickered and the man and the horse stopped.

Matt said, "Stand very still." The click was loud as he thumbed back the hammer of the carbine.

The man stopped. Only his eyes moved.

"I will see your hands," Matt said, "up beside your ears, you creeping son of a she-fox!"

The man's hands shot up and knocked his *sombrero* off so that it hung down his back by the chin string.

"You will come down here, slowly," Matt said, "and if you lower your hands, you will come down on your face."

The man worked his way down through the brush with bony wrists thrust high out of dirty shirt-cuffs. He was tall and thin and evil. A scar ran in a thin white line across his lips and up to the outer corner of his left eye, puckering the eyelid. He wore one gun. Matt took note of a thin rawhide string that encircled his throat and dropped down his back, under the shirt.

"My arms grow tired, friend, and my horse is walking away," the man complained.

Matt said, "Lie face down!"

The fellow complied awkwardly, because he dared not lower his hands.

"Now, *flaco*, unbuckle the gun belt, then roll over several times and lie still."

When the man had complied Matt ordered, "Take that string off over your head and lay the knife beside the gun."

Carefully, the man pulled the thong over his head and brought into view a dirk in a sheath, then rolled away from his weapons.

Matt stood and picked up the gun and knife and his own revolver. The squint-eyed man's revolver was a percussion-cap model no better than Matt's. Matt sat down cross-legged with the carbine across his thighs and said, "Now, talk!"

The man sat up, hunched his shoulders and spread his arms in a wide gesture.

"Accept my apology," he said. "I have made a mistake. I am looking for another man."

"What man?"

"Perhaps you have seen him, a damned *gringo*."

"Why do you want him?"

"My *patrón* . . . that is, a friend of mine suspects this *gringo* may be looking for him, with the intention of murder." His small eyes studied Matt. "Have you seen a man, bearded, dirty, a typical *Yanqui*, carrying one of those big buffalo guns?"

"Why should I have seen him?" Matt asked. "What have

I to do with this presumed *gringo* assassin, if such exists?"

"Well, they said at the Posada—that is, you stopped there yesterday—and two burro drivers, it is said, saw a rider on the road from Ojo Prieto. They did not describe him well, and I thought—well, if you have not seen him, I will be going." He started to get up.

Matt shifted the muzzle of the Henry half an inch, so that it bore on the man's belly. The man sat down again.

"Why should you think your *gringo* travels this way?" he demanded.

"Jesus Christ and various saints!" the squint-eyed one exclaimed. "Careful with that rifle! My friend, an importer of goods across the border, had some trouble with this *gringo* in Ojo Prieto. The *gringo* swore to kill him, so a watch was set on the *gringo's* house. Yesterday a rider left from that place and rode toward the river. The watcher was too far to recognize the *gringo*, but it is thought—the possibility is—"

Matt said, "Would a *gringo* be foolish enough to come down here where your friend has such fine friends as you, where he would be a marked stranger? No, your story does not hold water. I will tell you a better one. You were told at the Posada that a stranger had ridden past unaccompanied, with a poor horse, a good saddle, a better rifle and, perhaps, money. Your only thought is robbery and murder, and you are a liar."

The man snarled and half rose. "No man calls Jorge Ávila liar! You have my gun, or . . ."

Matt watched him sputter and subside.

"I call you liar," he said, "and stupid. You sounded like a bull buffalo on my trail. Thank Jesus Christ and various saints that you are still alive. Get up! Saddle my horse!"

Matt watched to see that the latigo of the cinch was well fastened. When the bay was saddled, he made the squint-eyed man lie down again. Then he threw the knife into the bushes, slung the captured gun belt over his shoulder, mounted, and rode up through the brush.

Squint-eye's horse had grazed back onto the flat land a way. It made no attempt to evade him. Matt caught the cheek of the headstall and took a Remington carbine from the saddle boot and dropped it onto the ground, then slashed the horse across the rump with the *romal* braided to his reins. It flinched and galloped off toward the road. Matt

smashed the breech of the Remington with a shot from the
Henry, and was almost thrown when the bay bucked in
panic at the shot.

When he had quieted the bay, he struck out for the cart
track and rode south.

For a while, he went with his face turned over his shoulder. To his right, to the west, the escarpments of the Sierra
Madre Occidental, the mother-mountains of Mexico, sloped
upward, rising as they marched south.

A little past noon, the road entered low hills which had a
luxuriant crop of *nopal* and organ-pipe cactus and *cholla*,
and nothing else. Around a wide bend, an emaciated dog
rushed at him, seemingly from nowhere, and snapped at
the horse's heels. Matt looked for the house. It was some time
before he saw it, a sorry shack inside a fence of living
cactus. The walls were of cobbles haphazardly supported
by twisted posts of *mesquite*. The roof was a thatch of
brush. Matt turned into the cart track that led to the shack.
An Indian woman in a shapeless garment, with coarse hair
hanging over her eyes came out and watched him approach.
Her anxiety was obvious.

Matt dismounted. "Favor of lending water for my horse?"
he asked.

The woman thrust out her chin in the direction of a well.
"Grácias." Matt thanked her.

He was at the well, holding the leather bucket for the
bay when he heard the squealing. It sounded like a hog
caught under a fence rail. The bay slung its head sideways
and knocked the bucket from Matt's hands. The screeching
continued and Matt saw the clumsy *carreta,* the great cart
hauled by two lean oxen, before he identified the sound:
wooden wheels turning on a wooden axle without benefit of
grease. The cart was a quarter of a mile away. It took them
ten minutes to reach the shack.

The driver jumped down and came hesitantly to Matt,
removed his ragged straw *sombrero,* and bowed. His ser-
vility was painful to see. There was fear in the black eyes
under the shock of graying hair.

"Señor," he said, "my house is yours." His Spanish was
so bad Matt could hardly understand the familiar formality.

"Is this the road for Cocatlán?" Matt asked.

"Cocatlán! *Sí! Sí!*"

"Is it far?"

"Sí señor! Lejano! Very far!"

"Well," Matt said, "how far, man? How many leagues?"

The man did not answer, but stood dull and confused.

"Is there something to eat?" Matt asked.

The man smiled suddenly, showing strong white teeth. He turned to the shack. *"Mujer!"* he shouted. There followed a string of explosive Yaqui of which Matt understood not a word.

The woman began to poke sticks and bits of charcoal under the flat, raised stone which served as griddle, then knelt and blew until thin smoke began to rise. While she slapped *tortillas* into shape and put some sort of meat to stewing, Matt helped the man unload a bushel or two of corn from the *carreta.*

The *tortillas* were good. Matt did not inquire into the antecedents of the meat, but dipped it up with pieces of *tortilla,* and tipped the clay bowl and drank the fiery liquor of the stew, and passed the bowl in his turn.

"You stranger," the Indian observed. "Travel far?"

"Well, yes," Matt said. "A matter of a strayed horse, a small stud marked with many spots. Have you seen such a horse?"

The Indian's eyes went opaque. He gazed out toward the *sierra,* and said nothing.

Matt reached into his jacket pocket and found a fifty-cent piece among the .44 cartridges. He laid it on the ground.

"For the meal," he said. "For your good hospitality."

He waited, but the Indian said nothing.

"Do you have a pistol?" Matt asked.

"Pistol, *Señor?* No. Much money for pistol."

Matt said, "I have an extra pistol."

The Indian looked into Matt's eyes for thirty seconds.

"A spotted horse was ridden past, three days ago," the Indian said. "Give me the pistol!"

"Do you think the horse is in Cocatlán?"

"Sí, Señor."

"The pistol is there on my saddle horn. Take the pistol only, not the belt and holster."

The Indian ran to Matt's horse and snatched the pistol. He thrust it inside his shirt, and came back to sit by Matt.

He reached for the fifty-cent piece. "I give corn for the horse," he said.

While the man put shelled corn into the saddle bag, Matt

filled the canteen. He put on Squint-eye's gun belt, shoved his revolver into the holster and mounted.

"Go with God, *Señor*," the Indian said.

"*Hasta pronto, amigo!*"

At the bend in the road he looked back. The Indian waved.

Chapter 9

THE TOWN was a cobbled street a quarter of a mile long and the ancient one-story adobes lined solid, like a wall down each side. There were people in front of a *cantina*.

Why don't they ever have a sign saying whatever the town is? How the hell does a man know where he's at! This could be Cocatlán, an' I better be careful now! That Indian, he said, "Very far," but he prob'ly figured that's what I expected to hear. Well, I'm here. And maybe Pecas is here.

Matt rode slowly down the street with a tight rein on the bay, which wanted to go sideways. How long since he had heard music like that? Matt began to grin and stopped his horse at the edge of the group in front of the *cantina*.

A young man in dirty white cottons stamped in the double-shuffle, with his hands clasped behind his rump and his sandals thumping on the cobblestones. The girl facing him swung from side to side in rhythm, holding out her full skirt and sawing it back and forth.

The musicians noticed Matt, and the music faltered. The dancers stopped, the onlookers stopped their stamping and handclapping and stared at Matt. He forced a grin and bowed low in the saddle. "Perhaps you celebrate a Saint's day in Cocatlán? I have been traveling, and I have forgotten."

A drunken *vaquero* glowered at Matt and snarled, "This is not Cocatlán! This is Río Seco, where we do not love strangers with green eyes!"

The *vihuela* player touched his shoulder and said, "Please, no trouble, Tibúrcio!" The man whirled angrily, and his hand went to the revolver at his hip. Two men grabbed him and hustled him out of the group. They, too, were armed, in contrast to most of the men in the crowd who carried only *machetes* stuck under belts or carried in leather sheaths.

The musician said, "I apologize for his crudity. It is no Saint's day, but the day of the weekly delivery of fresh *pulque* to the *cantina*. We of Río Seco celebrate the *pulque* each week more ardently than the Saints' days!"

Matt considered his role of footloose traveler, the role he must make convincing, and relinquished his urge to ride on. He grinned and said, "I will try this fresh *pulque*, but only if all drink as my guests!"

If some of them get drunk enough, he thought, I might hear some talk.

He dismounted. A small boy took the reins of the bay. Matt said, "Watch him for me, *chamaco!* It will be worth a peso."

"It will be a pleasure, *Señor*," the boy said. "None will bother him, nor the rifle, nor the saddlebags."

A small prostitute seized Matt's arm and, laughing, pulled him into the Cantina Violeta. The musicians were at their heels, and a crowd of perhaps thirty people—twenty-five men and five more prostitutes—came behind, pushing and laughing.

The fat, unshaven bartender bustled forward holding out a thick hand. "I am Vásquez, *Señor*. Welcome! How do you call yourself?"

"I call me Gómez," Matt answered, "Mateo Gómez, at your orders. And now, Señor Vásquez, let us try this *pulque!*"

Matt looked the room over. There were eight or ten men at bare pine tables, dimly seen in the dusk of the room. All but one seemed to be ordinary villagers or farmers. This one, at a corner table with a bottle of something other than *pulque*, was armed and had the arrogant look of the drunken *vaquero* Tibúrcio. Matt said, "Gentlemen, have the kindness to drink with a stranger!"

The bartender said, "What magnanimity! But, *Señor* Gómez, it pains me to suggest . . ." He rubbed a thumb and forefinger together.

Matt started to reach under his *camisa* for the moneybelt. He stopped the motion and said, "Do not be concerned, *Señor Cantinero*, but first, I have not dismouted since morning. Are there facilities, the *letrina*?"

"Out the door at the back, *Señor.*"

Matt walked through the open doorway in the back of the room and across a littered yard, to a privy against an ancient adobe wall. Inside, he relieved himself, then took a twenty-dollar gold piece from the moneybelt.

As he stepped back into the gloom of the barroom, he could see nothing at first, but heard the laughing jokes, the broad obscenities. He held up the coin.

"Serve these celebrants until the money is used up," Matt ordered. The room cheered in a burst of approbation as he gave the coin to Vásquez.

The proprietor kissed the twenty-dollar coin and yelled, "Ladies, get to work! And I do not mean your customary labors. Serve the guests!"

The five prostitutes ran back and forth amidst laughter and buttock-pinching, serving the bittersweet *pulque.*

Matt pulled a chair up to the table of the musicians. The *vihuela* player said, "*Señor,* are you an *aficionado* of Mexican music? Perhaps we may make some small return for your generosity—some ranchero songs?"

"How not?" Matt replied. "All my life—"

Quickly the musician said, "Of course! You are Mexican! How stupid of me! Well, '*El Arriero,*' perhaps?"

"A favorite," Matt said, and beat the rhythm on the table top and hummed, ". . . *pa' el cuello de mi chata, ay-y-y-y!*" and put the long falsetto on the end of it.

Dancers began to whirl among the tables and the drinkers all joined in the hand-clapping rhythm.

Much later, the tough at the corner table got up and brought his chair and his bottle to Matt's table. He said, grudgingly, "With permission," and the musicians shoved over to make room for him. The *vihuela* player lay slumped across the table with his head on his arms. The two other musicians took the guitar and the *guitarrón* and played endlessly in a corner, while the dancers stumbled and fell down, and some of the laughter changed to ugliness, and two *machete* fighters were thrown into the street.

The gunman belched and wiped spittle from his chin. His eyes were a little out of focus. He said, "I have not seen you before. You come from far?"

"I have been in New Mexico, but I left there for reasons of health, one might say. I have a cousin at Cocatlán, a companion of childhood."

Behind Matt, a grating voice said loudly, "Is your cousin, then, four-footed, with spots on his ass, and uncastrated, you son-of-a-whore?"

Matt stiffened, but did not turn his head.

"You filthy spy! I caught my horse! I talked with the Indian! I will castrate you here and now, and save Chuy the trouble!"

Matt dived out of his chair, hit the floor rolling, and came to his feet in a crouch. Knife in hand, the squint-eyed man faced him, the snarl on his face accentuated by the scarred mouth and puckered eyelid.

Matt feinted with his left hand toward Squint-eye's knife. Squint-eye twisted the blade to meet the feint. Matt hit him, right-handed, too high on the narrow forehead. The tall *vaquero* stumbled and went to one knee. He shook his head and braced himself for a lunging, upward slash.

Matt kicked him in the throat—on the bulging Adam's apple, and reached for his revolver.

The *vihuela* player half-opened bleared eyes and mumbled, "*Qué pasa? Qué pasa?*"

Matt's draw was slow. The holster was not tied down, and he had to grab it left-handed and tug at the pistol butt, and all the time he knew the surly bravo at the table would shoot him before he could get the revolver free.

He swung around with the revolver raised, and went slack with relief—the tough, drunker than he had appeared, was braced on stiff arms, leaning across the table to stare down at Squint-eye.

Squint-eye lay strangling. His open eyes showed white, glistening in the candle light, with the irises rolled up out of sight.

The altercation had aroused no interest. Everyone in the room was drunk, the villagers, the musicians, the prostitutes, even Matt a little, although he had drunk sparingly. He pushed his way out to the street.

The small boy said, "*Señor*, the horse is fine. No one molested."

Matt gave him a five-peso note and said, "Thanks, *compañero*." He swung up, let the bay have the quirt, hard, and went charging down the street.

The sharp night air helped to clear his head. Myriad stars made an upside-down, concave carpet overhead, its western edge cut sharply by the long black hump of the *sierra*. They told him it was midnight or later.

I wonder if I killed that squint-eyed bastard. Anyway he won't be riding tonight or tomorrow either.

Two hours out from town, he saw the glow of a low fire, off to the west of the road. He made out the star-silvered sheen of thatching, and under it the bulk of a small shack.

He stopped the horse and sat watching and listening. He could see a path running toward the shack. He touched the bay lightly with a spur and headed it up the path.

Instantly, a voice called, "Who are you and what do you want?"

"I am Gómez, a traveler. I have hunger."

He waited.

Presently the voice said, "Well, come ahead, and hold both hands high where I can see. Stop in the firelight and do not get down until I tell you."

Matt rode to the fire and stopped. Off to the right, the voice said, "Turn your mount's off side this way, so I can see the rifle, and take it slowly from the scabbard and drop it. Drop the pistol beside it, then move away and dismount."

When Matt had followed orders, an old man came out of the brush. His whiskers and eyebrows were white. He was barefoot, dressed in ragged *calzones* and *camisa*.

He said, "This is irregular. Tell me of yourself." He held a muzzle-loading, double-barreled shotgun. Its ten-gauge bores looked like twin cannons.

Matt said, "I ride to find old friends I have not seen for many years. I stayed overlong in Río Seco, and started late for Cocatlán. I ask the favor of a bite to eat and water, and perhaps a place to spread my *serape*."

The old man stood the shotgun against the adobe wall of the *jacal*. "Come and eat," he invited. "I, myself, have not eaten. I am goatherd, goats and a few sheep, and I have been after a stray. I am sorry for the incivility of the shotgun, but one does not know whether a stranger in the night may be a thief or assassin. You must be from very far, not to know, and to risk traveling alone."

"Well, I have heard some talk," Matt said, "but surely, a peaceful traveler, bothering nobody—"

"The more peaceful, the more easily robbed, *Señor*."

The old man indicated a place by the fire and placed two sticks on the coals. He stirred a clay pot with a wooden spoon and gingerly sampled the contents. "Whew!" he exclaimed. "I do not know which is hotter, the sauce or the heat from the coals. You like it hot?"

"I like it best hot," Matt said, "but first, with permission, I will unsaddle this nag and feed him."

Soon he was sitting by the fire, wolfing down mutton and savoring the blistering sauce of red *chilis*. There was green corn, small, immature ears roasted with the husks on, and onions burnt to charcoal on the outside but all sweet, hot succulence within.

"Is there then no authority, no soldiers to protect a man's honest rights?" Matt asked.

"There is no authority but that of murderers at Cocatlán, Chuy Medina and his assassins—Lázaro, the beast, and the others—the authority of rape and murder and terror."

"You speak plainly," Matt said. "Is there not risk that I may be one of Chuy's murderers?"

"No, I know them all," the old man said. "I will speak plainer still. Do not go to Cocatlán!"

Matt sat staring at him, and could think of nothing to say.

"You are a stranger in a place where strangers are rare and suspect. Chuy has boasted of stealing a spotted horse, and it is known how a *gringo* drove him and Lázaro out of the plaza at Ojo Prieto, in New Mexico."

Matt began to be scared.

"What has this to do with me?" he asked.

The old goatherd shrugged and said, "I will gossip no more, except to say one thing: I hate that son-of-the-great-whore, and I am not alone in this. It might be well for you to remember."

Chapter 10

THE FINE REEK of roasting meat woke Matt at the cold dawn. The old goatherd squatted on his heels before a small fire, tending twists of meat wrapped on small sticks, which leaned close over the coals. He said, "Good morning! Come and eat."

There was a brisk freshness in the air, and not yet any light. Far behind, only the highest, rugged peaks of the *sierra* were delicately touched by the first probing shafts of pale sun. Goats blatted behind the shack, in the brush corral still invisible in the dark cool shadows.

Matt sat up in the *serape* and rubbed his hands over the harsh stubble on his face and raked his fingers through his tangled hair.

"A fine morning, old one," he said.

He groped for the sandals and put them on. Only a little tenderness remained in his feet. He rose and folded the *serape* and went to squat by the fire.

"Take meat, friend, and here are beans in the pot, re-fried in mutton fat. I had no cheese, but the onions give savor." The old man spoke around a mouthful of hot meat. Matt helped himself, dipping into the bean pot with his skinning knife.

"Before I slept," he said, "I thought about what you said. Your advice is wise, but I am stubborn. I will go on to Cocatlán. Surely, if I mind my own affairs, I will meet no trouble."

"The danger is," the goatherd said, "not so much that you are stranger, but some might take you for *gringo*."

"*Gringo!* I?"

"It is not so much the green eyes," the old man went on, "and the clothing is authentic, and the horse and saddle, but there are other things—your feet, for example, with no callus on the sole and the toes cramped and misformed by the long wearing of boots. A foot accustomed to the *guarache* has the toes straight."

Matt resisted an impulse to sit on his feet.

"Well, I will tell you straight, old one," Matt said. "It is not altogether a casual search for cousins. There is a matter I must attend which is like an itch between the shoulders that a man cannot reach."

"One understands," the old man said. "They say that spotted horse is of quality seldom seen. Well, my goats are anxious. I must take them many miles each day, so they find enough. Ramos is not so much your friend as a hater of Chuy Medina. In case of need, remember Ramos, the goat-herd." He licked his fingers and stood up.

Matt rose and gripped the old man's hand. "I thank you for everything. And I will remember. How far is Cocatlán?"

"About twenty kilometers. And if you have seen Río Seco, you have seen Cocatlán. A wall and an arch and a street with adobes. But wait until night and go with caution. They say that, each night for a week, Chuy has tied a spotted stallion in front of the Cantina Palomar. There is one other *cantina*, the Bugambilia, but where the most noise comes out, that is the Palomar. Go with God, *Señor Gómez!*"

Ramos picked a frayed *gabán* from a peg by the door of the shack and settled the garment around his shoulders. He walked around the shack to his complaining goats.

Matt watered and fed the bay and checked over the Henry rifle and the old pistol. He made sure that the extra rifle shells and the spare cylinder for the pistol were still in the pockets of the jacket. A hobbled mule came in, but shied and went away when he offered it water. A rickety cart with loose buggy wheels sat behind the shack, beside an empty wooden tub. Matt wondered how far Ramos had to haul water.

He wandered into the shack and found the shotgun Ramos had aimed at him. There were no caps on the nipples. He thumbed the right hammer back, but there was no resistance —the spring must be broken. The barrels were London-twist damascus steel. A charge of powder equal to the load for his buffalo gun would open the breech out like a barrel with its hoops broken. There was a wooden ramrod in the ferrules under the barrels. The stock was split at the grip, and wrapped with a rawhide thong.

Matt dozed in the shade of the shack, and woke and looked at the angle of the shadow to check the time, then sat thinking.

What in the world am I doing a hundred miles down into Chihuahua, risking my neck for a horse! But maybe it will be easy—maybe I'll just find him tied in the dark, and lead him away and hit for the foothills and travel by night, the way we got away from Adobe Walls, and there will be no trouble.

The thought of Adobe Walls brought other thoughts, and he saw the spotted horse squealing with terror and Wohk Pos Its with a hole in his belly and his spine shot away. And he saw Buffalo Woman laughing, silhouetted against the snowy Big Horns in morning radiance, her frosty breath blowing thin smoke as she challenged him to race to the creek, and stripped off her dress and ran; and he, slower because of the fringed shirt and the leggings and breech clout, stripping naked to plunge, gasping, into the pool . . . and the shuddering run back to the honeymoon lodge among the pines . . . and the extravagant delight of the warmth of buffalo robes and the glowing fire pit.

Quickly he saddled the bay, mounted, harshly curbed it when it began to buck under the spur, and rode down the path to the road.

He saw Cocatlán from two miles away. Old Ramos was right. Go in after dark, and take no chance he didn't have to take. He turned off the road and made his way through great thickets of spiky *nopal,* and dropped down into a dry *arroyo* where flood waters had cut a steep-banked channel. There he waited for darkness.

When the sun was down he caught up the tie rope and jerked savagely when the bay shied. He bitted the horse roughly and swung up and spurred out of the *arroyo.*

As he rode, he made sure that the pistol was snug in the holster, the loaded revolver cylinder in his jacket pocket, and the skinning knife in its beautiful sheath flat against his tail bone, where his short jacket covered the handle.

It was nearly dark when he moved away from the road before it went under the arch at the end of Cocatlán's street. He dismounted and tied the horse to a bush.

At the arch he leaned against its brick surface, from which the plaster had eroded.

The afterglow of sunset lit the tops of the two facing rows of flat-roofed adobe houses. A few lights showed in doorways, and over one of them Matt saw a sign. He could barely read it—"Cantina Palomar." A girl leaning against the door frame turned her head and spoke to someone inside.

Matt chose the other side of the street and sauntered along. Women gossiped from the lighted doorways, their voices like music with the gutturals of Indian syllables or the liquid Spanish. A dog lunged from a doorway and, snarling, snapped at Matt's ankle. A woman screeched at it and seized it by the scruff of the neck. She spoke a shy apology and Matt answered, *"No le hace!"*—"Don't be concerned!"

Opposite the Cantina Palomar, he counted eleven horses standing at a hitchrack. There was one gray, gleaming pale in the dusk, but no chunky, small stallion with a spotted rump. The girl in the doorway called across to him, but he ignored her and strolled on.

Farther down, on his side of the street, the Cantina Bugambilia could boast only two horses at the rack. There was another girl in the doorway, a girl with a broad, Indian face, who smiled and spoke a lewd invitation, then called obscenities after Matt as he walked past.

There were no other horses in the town. Matt reached the far end of the street and stood undecided.

He sauntered back along the same side of the street. The Indian whore spat, "Eunuch! Boy lover!" as he passed. He went through the arch and walked to his horse. The bay shied as though Matt were some frightful ghost it had never seen before. Matt hopped with one foot in the stirrup as the horse circled, and cursed, remembering just in time to curse in Spanish. He laid the quirt hard across the bay's rump and curbed it when it tried to bolt. He held it to a walk and pushed it into the line of horses at the hitchrack in front of the Cantina Palomar.

The girl was still in the doorway. She asked, "Will you buy Trini a drink?"

Matt could see only a stretch of bare floor, a bar and a pockmarked bartender.

The girl reached for the rein. She smiled up at him, and he caught the glitter of a gold tooth. When he dismounted, the girl tied the bay and turned and took his arm. Her face was broad at the cheek-bones and, despite the flatness of the nose, had a half-wild beauty.

As they stepped into the light of a lamp on the bar and two kerosene lanterns smoking overhead, Matt turned again and looked at the gray horse and was suddenly sure. Some vague detail caught at his memory and turned it back to the Plaza at Ojo Prieto and a gray horse ridden by a fat, dirty Yaqui with filed teeth, and a roan horse carrying a slim Mexican. He hesitated, but the girl, Trini, tugged at his arm. He walked into a sudden silence, a pause, and a burst of renewed conversation.

"Buy Trini a drink, that she may toast your good health," she wheedled.

The bartender looked expectantly at Matt.

Matt said, "A *tequila* for me, and for Trini whatever she wants."

The bartender poured two *tequilas*. He pushed a small wooden box of salt within reach and said, "There is no lime."

Matt took a gold coin from his jacket pocket and handed it to the bartender, who examined it minutely.

"*Gringo* money," he said. "From Texas, perhaps?"

When Matt did not reply, the bartender pulled a cigar box from under the bar and dropped the coin in and brought out ten big, silver *pesos* and laid them in a row in front of Matt. He picked up one of the ten and dropped it back into the cigar box.

"One *peso* for the drinks and nine in change."

"You are pure bandit," Matt said, grinning to show that it was a joke. "Is the rate of exchange in Cocatlán only one for one?"

"If you wish to complain," the bartender said, "wait for the *patrón*. He will be here later."

"No complaint," Matt said. "I have been away in New Mexico for some years. I do not know the exchange."

He picked up the nine *pesos* and put them in his jacket pocket, put his back to the bar and leaned his elbows on it and surveyed the room.

Ten *vaqueros* sat drinking at bare tables. They looked at him, but no one spoke. These are no *campesinos*, Matt thought. Then he saw the fat man in the *charro* jacket with the big *sombrero* shading his face so the light gleamed only on the pointed teeth in the loose mouth. Matt drank the rest of his *tequila* and pushed away from the bar.

At his first step, Lázaro rose from his table and called, "A little moment, friend! Some trouble with the *cantinero?*" and came across the room.

Matt still might have tried to go, but Trini clung to his arm and said, "What, *guapo?* Not leaving? Stay with Trini!"

Lázaro, walking lightly for all his bulk, came up and faced Matt. Matt thought, if he knows me, I'll try for the pistol—or maybe the knife is better—I don't think he's seen it.

The Yaqui spoke in his bad Spanish, grinning all the

while. "You have a complaint? Tell me, I am *segundo* here."

"No, *Señor*, I but made a joke. I stopped for one drink, and now I must go."

"No, stay!" Lázaro urged. "We see few travelers—we bore each other here in Cocatlán."

Matt let his right thumb hook into the waist band, casually, back near the handle of the skinning knife.

"Come sit at my table," Lázaro insisted. "We will talk, and later Trini will warm your bed, for only two *pesos*. She is very good in bed. Is it not so, *consentida?*" His fat fingers reached for the girl's cheek and pinched so viciously that Matt saw pain flicker in her eyes. But she did not flinch.

Matt said, "Thank you, I must go," and stepped past the Yaqui and wondered if he would get through the door.

The only sound was the scrape of his sandals. He walked through the doorway. When he reached for the rein wrapped around the rail of the hitchrack, the bay snorted and lunged sideways and slammed into its neighbor. Matt wrenched its head down and got his toe into the stirrup and began the silly hopping on one foot, trying to keep his balance as the horse circled its rump away from him. He grabbed the saddle horn and hauled himself up and swung his leg over. The bay plunged in short circles, trying to get its head down to buck, but Matt hauled up on the rein and the horse backed, shaking its head. Hastily, Matt looked over his shoulder. In the doorway, Lázaro stood with his fists on his haunches, silhouetted against lamp light. Trini peeked through, under his arm, and faces gawked over his shoulder.

Matt said, "This *cagada* of a horse! Well, *adiós, Señores.*"

Lázaro snatched off his wide *sombrero* and slung it. It sailed under the bay's nose and the animal went straight up. Matt lost a stirrup, made a wild grab for the saddle horn, and fell off. The revolver jolted from the holster, and coins and the revolver cylinder spilled out of his pockets and rolled on the cobbles. The bay went plunging into the dark.

Matt sat up. He began to gather coins, and picked up the cylinder and reached for the revolver, hoping . . . hoping . . .

Lázaro planted a foot on the revolver and reached down and took Matt's arm. His thumb ground into the armpit, and Matt winced.

"Get up, buffalo hunter! Get up, thou *gringo* filth!" Lázaro hauled him up as though he were a child, and dragged him through the doorway, shouldering aside the gaping gunmen. He spun Matt and shoved him against the bar.

He snarled at the bartender, "Get Chuy!"

The man scuttled out.

Lázaro released the pincers grip on Matt's armpit and stepped back. He put the fat fists on his hips again.

"You almost fooled me, *gringo*! There was something, when you came in, something—then, when you went out, I saw the knife. The knife in that pretty Indian scabbard. And I remembered. You wore it that day in Ojo Prieto when you turned and crawled like a mongrel, and then shot from ambush."

Matt started to rub the sore arm pit, but the revolver cylinder in his right hand prevented him. He wondered if he could drop it and snatch the knife, but knew it was hopeless—he would never be fast enough, and the gunmen stood in a half-circle behind Lázaro and stared at him. Then Lázaro reached around and plucked the knife from its sheath. He stuck it under his belt and said, "Well, buzzard meat, we will wait. Chuy thought you might be crazy enough to try for the horse. He will be here soon."

There was a commotion at the door. Over Lázaro's huge shoulder, Matt saw a small figure appear in the doorway. She could not have been more than thirteen, and the paint on her child's face looked ghastly—two ill-considered spots of rouge against the coffee-brown skin. She minced into the room, clumsy in threadbare satin slippers that were too big for her, swinging skinny buttocks in a lewd caricature of seductiveness.

Trini, the whore, shrilled, "Regina! Go home!" and ran around Lázaro toward the girl. Lázaro shoved out an arm like a log of wood and stopped her. He grinned and bowed to the girl and said, "Come in, sweetheart, come in!"

The girl put her nose in the air and walked past Trini, saying, "If you can come here, I can come! Can't I, Lázaro!"

"Why, of course! Your sister is jealous because you are prettier. Come over to my table in the corner and—a little wine perhaps, or a few drops of *tequila*? This handsome stranger will sit with us and wait for Chuy. Chuy is going to entertain him." He took Matt's arm and pulled toward the table in the corner.

"Regina, little fool!" Trini screeched. "Go home! I will take a quirt to you."

Lázaro struck her with his elbow. "Get out of the way, *puta!*"

Trini snarled at him, "Thou lard-stuffed son-of-the-great-whore! I will slice thy fat throat, thou raper of children, thou foul carrion . . ."

Lázaro let Matt's arm go and swung a brutal backhand blow into Trini's face. She fell against the bar and stared at Lázaro's back. Her lip lifted in a snarl that showed the gold tooth.

Lázaro smirked at the girl and said, "Come, sweetheart! You, too, horse lover!" and reached for Matt's arm.

Matt swung from the level of his knees, his fist weighted with the revolver cylinder. He put his back into it and straightened his knees with a jerk, and felt flesh spatter, and the solid shock of his knuckles on bone.

The Yaqui straightened under the impact and all his joints gave away. He collapsed face down like a dead thing.

Matt felt the smash of a man's shoulder in the small of his back. He drove forward and fell, with someone's arms wrapped around him and someone kneeling on his kidneys, and both arms pinioned. The room was a pandemonium of shouting and hammering feet. Dazed, Matt was hauled erect and shoved against the bar and held spread-eagled.

A *vaquero* turned Lázaro over and knelt to mop his face with a wet cloth. Trini dragged Regina squalling to the door. There she slapped her, three full-arm swings with the open hand, and said, "Go home, thou baby bitch!"

Bawling, the girl stumbled out and Trini came back and pushed her way into the semi-circle of bravos around Matt.

Lázaro sat up and propped himself on his thick arms and shook his head. His jaw was swollen out past the folds of fat on his neck. His mouth was a smear of blood and his lower lip hung torn half loose. He rose and stood swaying and spat blood. He stumbled and went to one knee, and when he rose, the knife was in his hand. He mumbled, "Hold this filth still! Pull the *camisa* away! I will start at the navel, and cut slowly!"

In the sudden silence, a voice yelled, "Lázaro! Get back!"

Chuy Medina, the *gringo* hater, shoved his way through the bravos.

"What do you think you're doing, Indian? Who is this?"

Sullenly, Lázaro answered, "The *gringo* filth. The buffalo hunter of the spotted horse."

Chuy slapped him.

"I gave orders, thou hog! I told thee, bring him to me if he comes!"

He faced Matt and smiled. "Let him go," he said. "Would you like to see the stallion? He is at the hitchrack, outside. No? It will have to be something spectacular, perhaps a sharpened stake for you to sit on, unless I think of something better."

Matt went sick. God, I can't stand torture, not like a Cheyenne or a Mexican. If I can only rawhide him into makin' it quick—if I can get him mad enough . . .

He said, "Well, Chuy with the heart of *cagada*, you missed the fun at Ojo Prieto. After I shot the horn off your saddle, and you went away fast to pick splinters out of your belly, the whole town was laughing at Chuy, the gunfighter."

He spat at Chuy, and missed.

"They never laughed to my face," Chuy said, "not even that marshal, that *maricón*, Becker. And you were not laughing when you crossed the plaza—you stunk of fear. It was only from across the plaza that you dared face me, where you knew my pistol could not reach."

"Give me my rifle," Matt invited, "and you take one, and we will match skills out in the street, if you do not run as you did then."

"Anyone can kill with a rifle," Chuy replied, still smiling, "but only seven *gringos* have had the courage to face me with the hand gun. Perhaps you have heard—"

"I have heard that you are part Cholo and part rat and all coward," Matt said.

Chuy called him a name that was foul, even for Spanish obscenity, and snarled at Lázaro, "Put him against the wall, you and the bartender. I am going to break his arms before we put him on the stake."

Matt threw the revolver cylinder at him and lunged for the door. He almost broke clear, but Lázaro caught him and hurled him to the floor.

Matt hammered an elbow against the Indian's torn mouth, but the fat *charro* paid no heed. He dragged Matt to a table and grabbed his right arm in both great hands. Matt butted his bloody face, but Lázaro only shook his head and began to bend the arm across the edge of the table.

"I will break thy arms and legs and thy back and then thy neck, *gringo*!" He threw his weight onto Matt's arm.

Matt screamed as the bone snapped.

Trini threw the lamp.

It bounced from Lázaro's shoulder and burst with a crash of glass. Flame splashed across the floor. The shoulder of Lázaro's shirt was suddenly embroidered with a lacework of small flames, and he yelled and tore the shirt away.

Matt rolled from the table and fell heavily. He took his right wrist in his left hand and crawled on his knees. Bone ends grated, and he fought a wave of nausea. The room was a bedlam of yelling and running. A man tripped over him and went headlong.

In the uproar, Trini tugged his armpits and screamed, "Hurry! The back door! Get up!" She half-carried him. Lázaro's face wavered in front of him, a demoniac mask shouting unheard words. Trini slashed at the face with a knife. There was a hoarse yell.

Trini guided his stumbling steps through a back doorway.

Chapter 11

"Hurry!" Trini screeched. Matt could hardly hear her over the racket in the room behind. She went ahead of him, stumbled on something and turned to seize his right hand.

Matt went dizzy and fell against her. He grabbed his right wrist and could feel the displaced ends of bone—radius or ulna.

Trini seized his sleeve and pulled again. "Quick! The wall! There is a broken place, if I can find it." She moved left, and Matt staggered against rough adobe bricks.

"Here, the broken place!" Trini urged. "Pull yourself up!" She guided his left hand to a crumbled notch in the top of the wall. Matt tried to grip with both hands, and the pain shot up his arm like the rip of a knife.

"I can't do it!" he said.

"Look! Feel! I am stooping. Step on my back, Goddamn you! Hurry!"

Matt knelt on her back with one knee, carefully placed the other foot and stood crouching, braced against the wall with

his left hand. Trini swayed. Matt found the V-shaped break,
flung himself onto it belly down. Trini pushed him over and
he fell hard and came close to fainting. As he stood up,
holding his crippled arm, Trini tumbled down on him and
sent him staggering.

Across the wall, Chuy's voice squalled in the cluttered en-
closure, "You fat bastard! How do you know they came
out here?"

Lázaro growled, "I saw them."

"Pig head!" The blast of a heavy revolver shocked Matt's
eardrums. Once again, then twice more. Trini pulled him
down and clung to him.

"Lie still!" he whispered against her ear. "He's guessing!
Shooting into the shadows."

Chuy said, "They're not here, hog! Set Berto and Maldo to
searching the town. The rest will circle it. And we had better
find him, hog! *You* had better find him!" They went back
into the *cantina*.

Matt and the girl got up.

"Where can we go?" he demanded.

"I don't know. Nobody will hide us, and they are searching the town."

Over the crackling of burning rafters, Matt heard the hoofs
trampling the cobblestones of the street. His dizziness had
subsided, but the anguish of the broken arm was progressively
worse. Waves of dull, deep aching alternated with stabs of
torment.

"Trini," he said, "do you know that *arroyo*—the deep one
a kilometer north of the town, in that big *nopal* thicket? Can
you find it if we follow the road?"

"Yes, but they will be on the road, and the night is so
dark . . ."

"Listen, the night is dark for them, too. And if we stay
on the road, their passing will cover our footprints when
daylight comes."

It took them a half-hour of floundering through bean
fields and *milpas* to circle the town and find the road which
went north.

Three riders came at a hard gallop, the hoofbeats changing
abruptly from the staccato of the cobblestones to the muffled
thud of the earth road, as the horses swept under the arch
at the end of the street.

Matt calculated how much time they would have before the

horsemen overtook them, while Trini hissed at him and tried to pull him down beside the road. He saw the dim hump of brush, *nopal* cactus or *maguey*, ahead and to one side.

He pulled her to the clump of brush and they lay behind it. The riders charged past and the hoofbeats receded in an unbroken gallop.

"Come on!" Trini urged, and started to get up. Matt pulled her down and ordered, "Wait! Be quiet!" and strained eyes and ears back toward the arch.

Two dim shapes emerged, two men walking their mounts. They came, two blots in the dark, one on each edge of the road, peering into shadows, leaning to look down.

The two horsemen passed slowly, without a glance at the clump of *nopal*. Matt let his breath out slowly, and waited until the slow hoofbeats were nearly inaudible before he got up. Trini walked pressed against his left side until he shoved her away and said, "You are slowing us down."

In another half-hour, with no more alarms, she found the *arroyo* and led him to it, where its precipitous cut angled down from ground level. They made their way cautiously past the wicked spiked pads of *nopal* and the barbs of stunted *mesquite*. Matt said, "I should brush out our tracks, but I can't see them. I had that bay in here this afternoon, anyway —can't blot out all of it, and they'll search the *arroyo* as soon as it's light, whether we leave tracks or not."

They kept going for a half-hour, until Matt suddenly felt slack and used up, like an empty pemmican bag. He sat down and tried to feel the break in the bone of his forearm, but the swelling was too great, now, to feel it, and the light pressure of his fingers was added agony.

"Trini," he said, "cut two sticks, will you, about a half-meter long. Anything you can find. Then you can tear up my *camisa* for binding and we will splint this arm."

Wordlessly, she went off up the *arroyo*. For a while, he heard gravel rolling and the movement of branches. Presently, blundering in the blackness, she returned with two heavy, crooked sticks.

"I couldn't find straight ones. Are these all right?" She passed them to him. "Everything has thorns and everything is as hard as iron. I am afraid I nicked your knife."

"*My* knife?"

"I picked it up after you hit Lázaro for me. I knew you would need it. Also, I have this. You threw it, remember? And it hit the wall and rolled to my feet, and I put it in my blouse."

She put the cylinder of the revolver into his hand, the slung shot that had dropped Lázaro flat on his face—the cylinder loaded with powder and ball, with the hot little primer caps in its center hole—and as useless without the revolver as a revolver without a cylinder. He put it in his jacket pocket. It might be useful for starting a fire, the powder and the wax-soaked cotton around the primers.

"You have only one *camisa*," Trini said. "I have three petticoats."

He heard a ripping of cloth, then she said, "The strips are ready. Tell me what to do."

Matt said, "Lay the sticks one on each side of my arm, here on the ground. I will hold them in place with my left hand. Wind one of the strips just under my elbow, and tie it. Then the other just above the wrist. Wind them as tight as you can, even if I yell."

He drew a deep breath and pinched the forearm between thumb and forefinger, and thought he might faint. Under the swelling, he could feel the broken ulna. He gripped with his whole hand and put on all the pressure he could stand, and felt the sweat pop out on his forehead.

"Quick, put the sticks on!"

Deftly Trini bound and tied the strips of cloth. Matt lay back against the bank and let the breath go out of him, and for a moment, the black world whirled around him. Trini lay beside him and pulled his head to her breast and rocked him like a child. Under his cheek he felt the firm, soft swell of her breasts, slippery with his sweat, and the pulse of her round throat against his forehead. In five minutes, he was asleep.

Something, coyote or pack rat, went along the lip of the *arroyo* and knocked dirt down. Matt came wide awake, sat up, and knew instantly where he was. A bird rehearsed, somewhere near, and light had begun to show. Grimy and dishevelled, her blouse darkly wet with sweat where his head had lain, Trini sat up and rubbed her numb arm.

As though it might have come to him in sleep, Matt knew what he must do.

"There is a goatherd, Ramos," he said. "His *jacal* is twenty kilometers north, off to the east of the *sierra*."

"I know," Trini said, "he has been my client. For all his white hair, he has virility."

"I think he would help me," Matt said. "If you will go toward the foothills, get off the flat land without being seen. Be careful about crossing soft ground or wet spots if there are any . . ."

"We will get there," Trini interrupted. "Let's start."

"No, you go. This arm bothers me and I would slow you down. Besides, you will leave fewer tracks, less sign, if you are careful. Will you do this for me? Get him to drive the old cart with the mule, and put hay or corn stalks in it. I will not wait right here, I will find a place farther from the road, one where I can watch for him. It is a long way, I don't think he can come today. Tell him I will pay him, and tell him I need—"

"I know what you need," Trini interrupted again. "I will go now."

"Wait a minute," Matt ordered. "If no one is in sight, walk boldly out to the road, so the marks will be clear that you have left the *arroyo*. Then get off the road and strike for the foothills. Brush out your tracks with a branch where you leave the road again, and scatter sand on them. And Trini, thank you! I would be dead by now—"

"It is my life, too," she said, "since I threw the lamp at Lázaro—but that is not the thing. The thing is, you fought for me! When Regina came in and when you hit him and I saw his face break and his eyes turn up, and he fell on his pig's face, I felt the way I do when the priest comes and rings the little bell and burns the incense—as though I had a light shining inside of me. No one ever fought for me before."

Matt was startled.

What the hell makes her think I fought for her! All I wanted was to get out of there! Well, without her, I wouldn't have!

"Where will you go, Trini?" he asked. "You'd better not go back to Cocatlán. Could you get word to Regina, maybe have her meet you some place? You might go to El Paso, or up to Santa Fe—some place out of reach of those bastards —and maybe I'll see you again, in Santa Fe or El Paso . . ."

She looked steadily at him, as though something was hurting her. Tears welled into her eyes, spilled over, and rolled slow paths down her dirty cheeks. She turned and went down the *arroyo*, stepping carefully around the *nopal* pads.

"Wait," Matt said, and took a step after her.

She stopped and turned and her full, red mouth smiled. The gold tooth gleamed.

"You'd better leave me the knife," Matt said.

She took it from the waist of her skirt and threw it at his head.

The knife spun past him and rattled on the gravel of the bank. He stooped and picked it up. When he looked back, Trini was out of sight.

He stared at the empty spot where she had stood. There had been something in the set of her shoulders when she walked away, something forlorn and proud, too, that reminded him of the way Wo Ista had looked sometimes, when he had quarreled with her. He shrugged and picked up the remains of the petticoat she had torn up for binding his splints.

He began to wipe out the footprints, and the body prints where he and Trini had lain side by side. Then a thought struck him, and he walked down the *arroyo* where Trini had gone, planting his heels firmly and leaving clear tracks beside her light ones. The sun was about to rise when he reached the diminishing end of the *arroyo*. He studied the road in both directions. Trini was out of sight, and nothing moved. He climbed out of the cut and walked to the road, then started back, and carefully brushed out only his returning footprints with the cloth, dribbling sand over them, and scattering shriveled pads of *nopal*, small twigs and bits of dry grass on his trail. The sun burned into his back before he had made his way back to the shelter of the *arroyo*. There his progress was more rapid because he could step on water-bared rock and harsh, gravelly dirt that left no mark. Only where soft sand and silt lay and could not be avoided, did he repeat the careful disguising of his trail.

Some traffic began to move on the road, several riders, and a woman lazily keeping pace with a herd of goats while she made yarn with a twirling spindle and a wad of wool.

The pitch of the shadows on the steep bank told him it was about nine o'clock when he heard horses. He scrambled up to the lip of the *arroyo*. There was no mistaking the bulk of Lázaro on the gray horse. There was a thick, white bandage around his face. Three others rode with him at a slow

jog up the road. Matt slid down and looked back along
the bottom of the ravine. He had only made good a hundred
yards from the place where he had slept, but the *arroyo* was
so innocent Matt doubted even a Cheyenne would know he
had come along it. Perhaps a Yaqui would.

He lay and sweated and heard the horses as they slid on
their rumps into the lower end of the *arroyo*. Presently, he
heard voices.

"Lázaro, he came out. The tracks are plain. Trini, too."

"The tracks are *too* plain," Lázaro said. "Come on!"

Matt's glance explored the little area he could see. There was
no cover, only that last mass of cactus that almost blocked
the rough ditch, thirty feet back at a turn. The hoofs and the
voices came that far.

"Well, they lay there a long time," Lázaro said, "back
there where the rags were and the shavings of *mesquite*.
But I believe, now. He went back to the road. We will have a
look under the stone bridge by the *maguey* field up the road."

The horses turned, scrambling and knocking dirt from the
banks in the narrow place, and went back to the road.

An hour later, still painfully hunching along backward and
wiping out the marks of his passing, Matt came to a vein of
scab rock that intersected the *arroyo*. He climbed out and
looked back at the road. There was dust far to the north, but
nothing within sight. Stepping lightly, he made his way with
care to a branching maze of cactus that covered a half-acre,
and went into it, heedless of the thorns he could not
avoid. A dozen thorns penetrated pants, skin and muscle, and
broke off and stung like scorpions.

When he found a piece of bare ground in the thicket big
enough to stretch out on, he pushed his pants down around
his ankles and pulled thorns out of his thighs and shins. Then
he lay sweating, with his mouth beginning to swell from
thirst, and his right hand numb from the constriction of the
splint bindings, and an ache in the broken arm that had him
half delirious. Finally he loosened the bindings and retied
them, and the throbbing subsided enough to let him sleep.
The sun struck down as though each ray had pressure behind
it, and his face began to burn from the reflected heat, even
though he lay in the shadow of the cactus.

When the long, blue shadows began to pour across the flat
and lap up the slope to inundate the *nopal* thicket, he woke.
He weighed the advantage of approaching the road so he

would hear the cart if Ramos came during the night against the risk and labor of crawling back to the thicket before daylight, if Ramos did not come. Then he thought of the million spikes of thorn that would imprison him in the thicket after dark and prevent Ramos from reaching him, even if he called out and was heard.

In the last light, he made his way out of the *nopal,* doggedly accepting the bite of the thorns, and got down near the road. He lay supine, with his left hand under his head, his face fiery with sunburn, and his outstretched right arm pulsating with pain.

Chapter 12

RAMOS CAME within the hour. Matt lay still and waited until he saw the shape of flopping mule ears black against the afterglow over the *sierra,* then threw a handful of gravel which rattled on the side of the old water cart.

The mule broke into a spavined canter, but Ramos hauled on one rein and slewed the cart into the ditch and swung it in a short arc to reverse its direction. Matt walked down to it.

Ramos said, "Hold the reins a moment. I will see what I can do about those wheel tracks in the ditch." He leaned back and got a handful of corn shucks and got down. Matt took the reins and leaned against a crazy wheel.

Stooping, Ramos spent a long time brushing at the marks of hoof and wheel, and came back to the cart. "I don't know," he said. "Maybe that will do it, but in the dark I cannot be sure. Get in the cart bed and I will cover you."

Matt lay down in the cart. It was too short to permit stretching out, and he knew the jolting ride would be a nightmare. Ramos covered him with corn shucks, then sat on the front edge of the cart bed and flapped the reins on the mule's back. The cart wobbled rhythmically on its dished wheels, and thumped even when there were no bumps, because the wheels had flat spots.

Ramos handed back a goat skin of tepid water and a piece of jerked meat. Matt drank, and drank again, and tried to chew the meat. His mouth was too sore with the sunburn and the swelling from thirst. The cart jolted him and bounced him, his arm ached dully, his burned lips smarted, and he went to sleep.

The wracking of the cart woke him when Ramos turned from the road onto the rock-strewn track that led to his shack. When the cart stopped, Trini was there, silent in the dark. She helped Matt down and held him close when he stumbled on his benumbed legs.

He sat down by the cold fire-pit and stretched out on his back. The night was still black, and he had no idea what time it was.

Ramos said, "Sit up, Gómez. You cannot rest yet. Eat a little, then you and Trini must hide."

"Are they looking for me?" Matt asked.

"Lázaro, this morning, then Chuy with three men, this afternoon, just before Trini got here. He made threats and offered me money, but I did not know what he meant."

"I saw him come," Trini said. "It was lucky. I had just got here, and I was waiting in the brush for this old one to appear."

"I was in the brush corral," Ramos said, "caring for a couple of my she-goats which were about to give birth—Anastasia and Virginia. They both had fine kids. I have built a brush shelter in the corral, a *ramada* for them to get out of the sun. Now you and Trini must get hidden—it is only two hours until dawn."

"You think they will come back?" Matt asked. "They have been here. Why should they come back?"

"The place on the road where I found you, the tracks, they will find it. They will track you up that *arroyo* where you hid, too."

"But," Matt protested, "I erased the tracks there. I am no city boy. I have lived with Indians."

"You have not lived with Yaquis."

"They won't read that trail," Matt insisted. "But, if they do, old man—in the *arroyo* and the wheel tracks by the road —it will bring them here, to you. You should have thought of the risk, if you are so afraid of Yaquis."

"I did," Ramos answered. "Now eat. We waste time."

Matt suddenly felt humble. He wanted to say something, but could find no words.

He gulped down cold beans and *tortillas*. Ramos wrapped

more in corn husks, and gave them to Trini, and filled the
water bag. He said, "Come on, now. You must stay hidden
until we can find a way to get you out of Mexico, or until
they give up the search. I must have time to wipe out all marks
here around the *jacal*. Trini and I fixed a place to hide you
before I went for you."

"I hope it is not far," Matt mumbled around a mouthful
of *tortilla*. "I am about done in."

Old Man Ramos said angrily, "*You* are done in! You have
slept in a *nopal* thicket all day and in my cart half the night!
Trini walked twenty kilometers of *nopal* thickets and brush!
Her sandals are worn out and her feet are bloody! I have
heard no word of thanks from you!"

Suddenly Matt was angry.

"By the blood of Christ! She had her own neck to think
about! You think she did this for me? She did it for her own
whore's hide! It is *you* I must thank, and I have no words to
do it."

He got up and Ramos grabbed his sore arm and whirled him
around and grated, "Listen, *gringo!* Who threw the lamp
and dragged you out of that *cantina* and saved your miserable
life? I will turn you out on the road and let Chuy have you!"

Matt felt as though some one had kicked him in the guts.

"Trini . . . Trini . . ." He pulled her close and put both
arms around her and ignored the stab of pain in his wrist.
She put her face against his stubble and hugged him and did
not speak.

Ramos pushed him lightly. "You were not expected to
think, with the *cantina* burning, and your arm broken, and
those wolves trailing you up the *arroyo*. The hiding place is
only a few steps away, in the brush corral, a hole we dug
under the *ramada*, with poles across it. And there will be
muck, and goat manure spread over the poles, and Anastasia
and Virginia and their new babies tethered alongside. Everything will be so uncomfortable and smell so foul that even
Lázaro's Yaqui nose will not smell you out."

It was as Ramos had described, a shallow hole scooped out
against the brush wall of the corral, under the shelter of the
brush *ramada*.

Trini and Matt got in. There was barely room to lie side
by side, and no head room for sitting.

When Ramos had laid the poles over it and scattered
mouldy hay on the poles and tied the two she-goats near, he

said, "If they come, they will not look for you close to the *jacal*. They will beat the brush and look for tracks. I will go out with my goats, as always, and not come back until night, so they will see no change in my habits. This is the best we can do."

They heard him go away and close the creaking gate of the corral.

Trini wriggled and turned and got on her back. He was aware of the discomfort of her elbow jabbing his chest, but more aware of the warmth of her rounded hip against his belly. He achieved a fairly comfortable position for the broken arm, and relaxed. The she-goats shifted about and the kids blatted and suckled, almost overhead.

Trini said, "This is the first time I have lain quiet beside a man, and I do not even know your name. How do you call yourself?"

"I call me Mateo Gómez. But I am not truly Gómez," Matt explained. "My mother was Gómez. She was half *gringa*. I am really Fletcher, and I am mostly *gringo*. Chuy stole a fine horse from me in New Mexico, and I came to get it back."

"He boasted of the little spotted stud, and how he had taken it from a cowardly *gringo*," Trini said. "It was a brave thing to come for it. Chuy has killed for lesser reasons, even for no reason at all, except to show his skill with a revolver."

Matt shifted his shoulders, and dirt trickled down his sweaty neck. The pain of the broken wrist was less, but the hand below the splint was swollen and felt hot. A headache had begun to gnaw at the base of his skull.

"We had better stop talking," he said. "We are supposed to be hiding."

"All right, Mateo." She kissed his cheek and whispered, "But it was wonderful of you to fight Lázaro when he hit me. I am only a whore, but you fought for me."

She lifted her head and pulled his left arm under it and settled back. Early dawn filtered down through the poles and scattered hay, and mottled her face with pale light. The long lashes lay sweetly against the curve of her brown cheek.

She looks like some mission school kid, Matt thought. Poor little devil, I can't set her straight about why I slugged Lázaro.

All the knots in his nerves unraveled, and he slept.

The sun stood well past noon when he awoke, confused and hot. The ache in his head was almost as bad as the one in his arm. He muttered and Trini's sweaty hand came hard over his mouth.

Then he heard the horses walking close past the brush corral.

A man said, "Nothing in there but those goats."

Matt recognized another voice, Chuy's—"If they're here, they'll be in the brush, not close to the *jacal*. Things do not look right by the shack. Ground swept too clean. More and more, I do not trust Ramos. If he has helped the *gringo*, I will wrap him in wet rawhide and let the sun squeeze the guts out of him. He went somewhere with the cart last night. And Lázaro found some of Trini's tracks in the foothills. They might have been pointing here, but he could not tell. Let's beat the brush."

For nearly an hour, Matt and Trini lay in sweating tension, hearing the calls and the thrashing of brush back on the hillside. Then the horsemen went away. As soon as they had gone, Matt sat up, shoving the poles aside with his head. Trini tried to pull him back.

"Wait, Mateo! They will hear! What is the matter?"

"Got to get out," he muttered. His head felt as though it were close to a fire, and his right hand felt as though it were in one. He tried to flex the fingers, and a hot wire ran up his arm along the nerves, clear to his shoulder.

He stood, scattering the poles, and swayed drunkenly. The kids ran across the corral and the she-goats pulled at their ropes. Trini rose to her knees beside him and looked fearfully toward the road.

"Mateo, what is the matter? Are you sick?"

"I don't know. My head—" He climbed out of the hole and lay down.

Trini tugged at his arm. "Mateo! Get up! We will go into the brush. We can't stay out here in the open!"

He rose, slack-kneed, and leaned his weight on her. She staggered under it, and they made a zig-zag course into the shelter of thick *mesquite,* where Matt collapsed.

Trini laid her hand on his forehead. "You are burning," she said. "I will get water. I wish Ramos would come."

Matt realized that she had gone, and did not care and did not hear her return. After a while he roused when she took his head in her lap and poured water from the goatskin into his mouth. His arm and hand still ached, but the bursting pressure no longer pounded at wrist and fingers.

"I took the splints off." Trini said, "Do not move it."

He fell into troubled sleep, soothed by the caress of Trini's hand on his forehead.

Voices woke him, down by the shack.

He saw that stars were brilliant. He was alone.

"He would not stay in the hole, then . . ." Trini was saying, and old man Ramos answered, "Well, so long as nothing happened. But it was a bad risk."

"His head is on fire with fever," Trini said, "and his hand is swollen, and dark red. I took off the splints, because I thought the blood . . ."

"Can you bring him down here?" Ramos broke in. "I will risk a fire for light. There is no time to lose. I must splint the arm again. It must be done, even if it swells."

Matt stood up. His broken arm hung like a pulsating pendulum. He walked to the shack, light-headed and dizzy.

With flint and steel, Old Man Ramos was knocking sparks into a wad of dry grass at the fire pit.

He looked up and did not smile, and said, "I left the goats to fend for themselves, and went to a place where I could look down to the place where I met you last night. Lázaro and others were there, looking for tracks. It was getting too dark for them to see much, so maybe we have a little time. But they will be here."

Ramos blew on the smoldering grass and added bits of charcoal. He said, "Let's see that arm."

Matt sat beside him, and Ramos took his hand and kneaded it gently. Matt ground his teeth and sweated while the old man felt the swollen forearm.

Ramos said, "The circulation was cut off too long. We will use rawhide binding for the splint this time. It will pull tight as it dries. Then, if it is too tight, you can wet the rawhide and it will loosen. That is, if you do not run out of water where you are going."

Trini came back from the water barrel with a bulging goatskin.

"Trini, bring the shotgun," Ramos ordered. "It is behind the door."

She put the water skin down and got the gun.

Ramos cut the rawhide thong that was wrapped many times around the split stock of the gun, and put the stiff coil into a jar of water to soak. He smoothed two sticks with a machete, then slit the right sleeve of Matt's jacket.

"We will put the splints over the sleeve of the *camisa*," he explained. "Then you can take the jacket off when you wish."

The fingers were fat, like sausages, and discolored as though bruised. The palm was puffed and the knuckles dimpled. Trini washed the forearm and hand, and tried gently to smooth the indentations where the splints had pressed. The tepid water felt like a suave unguent, but Matt could hardly stand the rubbing.

Ramos bound the splints with wet rawhide. "Trini, there is a flour sack in the *jacal*. Pack any food you can find. I will get the mule."

Trini took a torch and rummaged in the shack. Ramos brought the mule and bridled it, and tied the water skin and the sack of food together and slung them over its withers.

"Trini," he said, "sit in front, and Mateo can sit behind and hold onto you. Do you know where the big mesa is, the one near the pass where the trail to Bacanora goes through?"

"I herded sheep there when I was a little girl," Trini said. "But that is back almost to Cocatlán!"

"It does not matter how close to Cocatlán," Ramos insisted, "so long as you stay hidden until some escape presents itself. That mesa is the only place that has water, a spring near a cleft in the rock," he said. He picked up the shotgun. "Too bad this is useless—there are no percussion caps."

Matt said, "I have six caps packed in a revolver cylinder. Here, take it out of my pocket."

"I meant for you," Ramos explained. "Even if Chuy learns I am involved, I cannot fight him with one load of birdshot. But if his men scatter out to track you and one alone should find you, it might give you a chance. Here, Trini, take it."

He went into the shack and came back with a small package of corn husk. "Here, Mateo, is powder and shot, perhaps two loads, all I have. Remember, only the left barrel functions on the gun."

Matt put the package in his jacket pocket. He stood up

and said, "What of you, old man? If they come here—if they think you have helped me, it will go hard."

"I will insist I have never seen you. At first daylight, I will wipe out all the marks and fill in the hole in the corral."

Trini climbed onto the mule and pulled her skirt down to cover her thighs. "Pardon the immodesty," she said.

Ramos got an old blanket from the shack and gave it to Trini, then helped Matt to mount behind her.

He said, "Try to get to the canyon that leads to the mesa by daylight. If Mateo is able then, turn the mule loose and walk the last kilometer, and be careful about leaving tracks. The mule will come home. Well, go with God!"

He went down the track to the road.

Trini clucked to the mule. It moved up the hill, picking its way carefully among boulders and brush. Each jolting step transmitted waves of pain down Matt's arm. His face grew hot again, and his thoughts confused. Once he started to sing a Cheyenne love song, and Trini told him to shut his mouth.

At last the black changed to charcoal gray, then to smoke blue, and blurred shapes of bushes and rocks swam past. Trini slid off and said, "Get down, Mateo. I think I know where we are. We will sit here until it gets lighter."

Matt just sat there with his head whirling, and she spoke sharply and pulled at his foot. When he understood and leaned over, he would have fallen if she had not taken most of his weight.

As far peaks caught patches of pale rose, Trini recognized the mesa which was their goal. They had passed it by half a kilometer.

Trini dragged the water skin and the food bag from the mule's back and set them down. She put the blanket over her shoulder and the shotgun under her arm, then looped the rein over the big hammer-head and said, "Go home, mule!" The mule shambled away down the slope.

Trini said, "We have a hard climb, and we must hurry, before full daylight comes."

"Let's rest," he pleaded. "Just a few minutes, Trini."

"No! Get up!" she demanded, and when he did not move, she kicked his shin. Matt got up and looked at her. She was haggard. The great black eyes stared at him from dark circlets. Matt remembered that she probably had not slept the night before and perhaps not during the day. He took the water and food bags and slung them across his shoulder.

"Are we going up that slope?" he asked, and nodded toward a steep, high slant, carpeted with the boulders of a big rock slide.

"The spring is somewhere above it," Trini explained. "There is a wide bench with juniper and young pine, and at the far side is the spring. But we had better circle the rock slide."

"We'll go up the slide," Matt said. "No one will think we have gone up it if it looks too hard."

They walked to the talus fan of the slide. Matt started up, choosing each step with care, testing rocks with his hand to see if they were solid, and not looking back and not stopping for nearly an hour. Trini stayed close behind. He could hear her labored breathing. At last, he attained the top of the rock slide and fought for breath, too tired to reach a hand to Trini and help her up the last muscle-quivering step.

"We will rest here," he said, "before we climb this last slope."

Trini was the first to recover breath and a measure of strength. She picked up the water bag and said, "We had better keep going."

Matt slung the food sack over his shoulder. "The rock slide has broken our trail and the hill is too steep for horses," he said. "I do not think they will search it."

Trini started to climb. "There is an easier way up, though," she said. "It is a favorite place for pasture, especially with the spring there."

The dry grass was as slippery as ice. The food bag weighed a ton, and swung and bumped and got in his way. The bad arm ached and once, when he slipped and came down on it, he cried out in pain and fought nausea before he could go on.

They achieved the top of the mesa and lay panting, dull-eyed and silent. The mesa stretched grass-grown between clumps of gray-green juniper and blue-green pine. At its far side were water-carved *arroyos*, the vanguard of the impassable mountain declivities beyond.

"Where is the spring?" Matt asked.

"Across the flat. I will show you."

The site of the spring, at the foot of a bare upthrust of rock, was embossed with a thousand footprints—deer, javelina, coyote, lion, quail, burro, sheep—all baked hard into the bisque of dry earth, and there was no water.

They plodded along the meandering line where the hill debouched onto the bench a quarter kilometer from the spring, and Matt saw a place that would serve. There was another talus fan of earth, stones and rock from another ancient slide. On its slope, great boulders had been partially covered by subsequent slides of earth and smaller rocks. Two massive boulders ten feet apart, leaned together at their tops and were partially covered by a great broken slab, to which clung a stunted juniper.

"That will do for now," Matt said, pointing. "Good shelter, and we can see the whole bench, and no one can climb up the slide without noise. Don't leave any footprints, step on the rocks."

He climbed to the dark opening and tossed a stone inside awkwardly, with his left hand. There was no angry buzzing, and no diamond-backed horror slithered out.

"Welcome home, Trini," Matt said.

Chapter 13

MATT SPREAD the blanket on the tilted earth that made a kind of floor between the boulders, and she went to it on hands and knees and slid down full length. He looked down at her, at the full mouth still bruised from Lázaro's elbow smash, at the tangled hair dull with dirt and the small, high breasts with the sweat-drenched blouse clinging like skin. Again, he thought how innocent she looked—and still, she's tougher than bull hide, and she's a whore. She didn't cry when that Yaqui hit her, but she cried when I talked rough to her, and I haven't got the heart to tell her it was just my own skin I was fightin' for, not hers.

He took off the jacket, swearing when the movement sent a spasm of pain through the broken arm. He knelt clumsily, took the revolver cylinder and the coins and rifle bullets from the pockets and folded the jacket.

"Here, Trini, raise your head."

She stared at him uncomprehendingly for a moment, then lifted her head while he slipped the jacket under. He rose and looked out between the boulders at the mesa top. He studied the talus below the boulders and could see no place where they had left tracks in climbing. He went back and lay beside Trini. She did not open her eyes, but took his hand and held it to her breast and was instantly asleep.

Coyotes woke him, caterwauling down on the grassy bench. There was a smell of dawn. He was shivering, and when he moved, Trini muttered and snuggled against his back, but did not waken. Only his right hand was not cold, fat below the binding of the splints. He put it against his whisker-harsh face and felt the fever heat of it.

He got up and found the water bag and drank deep. The food sack held a mixed-up mess of boiled beans and soggy *tortillas*. He ate a little, but was soon satisfied.

As daylight came, he went carefully down to where the bench leveled off, and looked back at the boulder shelter. Scrubby junipers almost hid the bottom of the opening —there would be no need for excessive caution so long as he and Trini stayed inside. He turned to study the bench. Jack rabbits wandered across it and a buzzard sailed a vast, wing-tilted circle in the faultless blue. He began to walk across the mesa, careful to step only on hummocks of dry grass and half-buried stones.

At the edge of the declivity he lay and watched the road far below, but could see no traffic. Returning, he followed the perimeter of the top of the mesa and came upon a trail with old goat and sheep tracks and small, neat prints of burro. No one had brought stock up here since the spring had gone dry.

Trini watched his slow climb back to the shelter.

"I woke up and you were gone," she said accusingly. "I was afraid you had left me."

He sat listlessly against the slanted boulder.

"The rawhide on the splints has drawn too tight," he said. "My head aches."

"Let's take the splints off," she said. "I will pad your arm with cloth."

She took his skinning knife and gently cut the bindings. The relief was immediate. In a few minutes, the returning circulation made the fingers ache as though they were being hammered. Trini turned her back and raised her skirt and murmured, "Excuse me," then took off a petticoat. She turned with an odd look on her face.

Well, I'll be damned! She's embarrassed! Matt choked back an impulse to laugh.

"Soon I shall be naked if that arm does not get better," she said.

She tore strips from the petticoat and wrapped them onto the swollen forearm, then bound on the splints securely, but not too tight. Matt wiggled the fingers and felt only firm, even pressure.

Trini pulled a handful of wadded *tortillas* from the sack. "What will we do, Mateo?"

Matt replied, "I don't know. There has been no time to think. For now, all we can do is wait and be careful with the water and food. Surely they won't hunt long just because I hit Lázaro. When they quit, we'll get out of here."

"You don't know them," Trini said. "You are *gringo*. They will not quit. You have shamed Chuy twice, in Ojo Prieto and then in Cocatlán, with his men looking on. He had you caught, and you got away. It is a matter of his pride."

"Well, all right. I believe you. But *you* can go, after you are rested. Where are your parents?"

"My mother is dead. My father was killed along with Chuy's father and brothers in the ambush near Ojo Prieto. He was Mora, a cousin of Chuy's father. I am Trinidad Mora."

"There must be somebody you can go to."

"There is an uncle, a drunkard, in Chihuahua. He is religious, and I am whore. He would not take me in."

"Well, take some money, then. Travel by night. Go across the border, anywhere, if you think Chuy and Lázaro will still be looking for you."

She gave him a look he did not understand.

He waited for her to reply, then shrugged and said, "When this quiets down in a day or two, I am sure Ramos will come. He might even bring horses. With horses, we can get away. That is our big need. We will just rest and wait until he comes."

For two days they stayed in the shelter, leaving it only for bodily relief. Matt tried exercising fingers and hand, but there was no strength in the hand nor grip in the fingers, and the movement was too painful. He carried the arm in a sling made from the remains of the sacrificed petticoat.

During daylight hours one or the other watched the flat ground and the place where the sheep trail would give easy access to horsemen. Nothing untoward occurred, nothing to cause alarm. Matt considered building a fire against the chill of night, but was afraid it would be smelled, or that reflection on boulders would be seen afar. So they huddled together during the dark hours and Matt, as he began to recover from exhaustion, was more and more aroused by the small breasts, the warm little belly, and the round thighs that pressed against his back or side throughout the night.

In the afternoon of the second day, the fever was gone from his head, and the inactivity and the quiet began to get at him. Abruptly, he rose. "I'm going to have a look at the road, see if anything is stirring," he said.

He descended the slope carefully, and went across the mesa, glad to be moving. Nothing moved on the road. Circling back along the perimeter, he examined the old goat trail and found no fresh tracks.

He climbed from rock to rock back to the boulders and came around the scrub juniper that screened the shelter.

Naked, her back to him, Trini squatted dabbing at her feet with a moistened rag. She was so preoccupied she had not heard him approach.

Matt turned his head away and felt the heat of embarrassment in his face. He had some confused idea that he should tiptoe away. Then he turned and gaped at her.

She rose gracefully from her squatting position. Her beautiful, damp body took on highlights like old, polished bronze in the gloom, the waist slender, the shoulders delicate and sloping, the small buttocks round and solid above the tapering columns of calf and thigh.

His heart began to thump.

Some small sound warned her. She turned, crouching, and stared.

Her unmistakable alarm, and the animal grace of her movement kindled a sudden heat of lust in Matt. His chest felt tight, his breathing rasped hoarse through his open mouth. He lunged for her. She tripped backward and fell on the blanket.

"Trini . . . Trini . . ."

His bearded chin ground into the sweet hollow where throat joined shoulder. His hand slid over the resilient 'softness of belly, feeling the muscles contract, and he tried to shove his knee between her clamped thighs. He raised his head and pushed his mouth onto hers.

Trini got a hand under his chin and squirmed from under him like a coiling snake. As she rolled away she snatched the skinning knife from the sheath at his hip.

Squatting like a small enraged beast, she snatched her skirt and held it across her breasts and called him vile names.

Matt stared at her in total disbelief, with the flush of anger beginning to stain his stubbled face.

Trini fell silent and dropped the knife. She wrapped the skirt around her body and stared back at him. Her eyes began to glisten, huge and black, and two fat tears slid down her face.

Matt said, in English, "Oh, for Christ's sake!" and got up. The bad arm was aching. He started to walk to the opening.

Trini said, "Mateo?" uncertainly. "A little moment—wait!"

He stopped but did not turn, and heard the rustle of clothing. He was pretty confused. Except Wo Ista, the only women he had known were the dance hall whores, who carried on their trade in the deadfalls of the shipping towns on the prairie, or the wives of hide buyers or businessmen. The first expected neither respect nor consideration and were tougher than the buffalo skinners and trail drivers they serviced. The others were untouchable and their pedestals were high.

Trini said again, "Mateo?" and took his hand and made him turn around.

Desire had been shocked out of him. The black eyes looked up at him beseechingly. She straightened the skirt and tucked in the grimy blouse.

Matt sat down, his back against the slant of the boulder, and she sat across from him and said, "You think—you think because I am whore . . . ?"

"Well, aren't you? Goddamn it!"

"Yes, Mateo. But not really. Not inside."

Matt laughed, short and ugly. "Lázaro has had you, and all the town of Cocatlán," he said bitterly. "Even Old

Man Ramos. But you're too good for Matt Fletcher, the *gringo!*"

"Oh, no! No!" she cried. "Mateo!"

She blew her nose on the hem of her skirt and began to talk, while Matt sat and sifted dirt through his fingers.

"How would I live, Mateo? I have eighteen years. Since fourteen, I have no family, only Regina. No man to take my part when men say dirty things to me and try to get their hands on me. But even then, when I was trying to keep a few goats and grow a little corn I was forced. Chuy took me to the back room of the *cantina*. And I had to pretend it was all right, or it would have been worse. The whole town knew about it, but even after that, there is a boy, a *vaquero* on a ranch, who wants to marry me. But he is afraid of Chuy and I only see him when he comes to the *cantina* and takes me to the room and pays the two *pesos*."

Matt did not want to hear any more, but Trini went on, in a rush of words . . .

"And then, Lázaro. He was afraid to do it before Chuy tired of me. That is the only thing that stopped him, before—he did not dare because of Chuy."

"Couldn't you go away?" Matt asked.

"Where to, Mateo? All the towns are the same for a girl. There is no way for a girl to earn money, only the *cantinas* and the cribs. Some get rich, too, the pretty ones who do not become drunkards or get syphilis. And I was afraid for Regina. She thought it would be fun in the *cantina*, and then Lázaro came smelling around."

"Well, I guess you couldn't help it," Matt said. "But why, then, this afternoon, when I . . . ?" He did not quite know how to put it.

"But that is just it!" she said. "In one part of my life I am whore, but in my heart I am not. And it is all right, because one accepts what God sends. I confess and say the Hail Marys and buy candles, and it is all right. For money it is all right, and because I must do it. But in that other part of me, I am clean, and not whore. When Lázaro hit me, you fought for me. I would be a good woman for you and never look at another man. And the part of me that is not whore, no man can have me just because he needs a woman. I will kill him first! Or me! I will kill me, too!"

Matt got up and went to sit beside her. He put his arm around her and said, "I am sorry, Trini. I will watch myself, but you have to help. This sleeping together and undressing and all that . . ."

She began to cry. She slid down until she was on her back, and pulled him onto herself and began to fumble at the waist of his leggings.

The mating was so wild that it was equally she taking him. But even in his frenzy, he was shocked by the fierceness of her desire.

And after, as he lay spent and replete she kissed him gently and said, "That is the *first* time! The first time for me, do you hear? And now, I am your woman!"

Matt lay shaken and confused and had no answer. His mind went inevitably back to Wo Ista and the honeymoon lodge among the aspens by the frozen river—and the memory of Wo Ista was almost too much to bear. She, too, had been fierce and passionate, but with a sweetness like music.

He sat up with his back against the boulder and said, "About you being my woman, it won't work."

She raised her head from his knee, her eyes wide. "You are married?"

"No. Well, in a way, but that's not what I mean. I don't want *any* woman. I came down into Mexico for my horse, if I can get it. If I can't, I'm going back. That's all!"

Her mind had fastened on just one phrase. "Who is she? Do you love her? Is it some *gringa*?" Her voice was small.

"No, nobody. I'm not married."

"Then I am your woman," she said, and smiled and settled her head on his knee again.

"Damn it, no! You're all right, and you've helped me a lot. And we still have to help each other. But when we get out of this, I'm going back to New Mexico."

"All right," she agreed. "We will go."

He had to struggle to suppress his exasperation. He cast about in his mind for some argument which she must accept, but which would let her down easy.

"What about Regina? Would you go away and leave her?"

She was silent for some time. Then she said, "Regina will do what she will do, and I cannot stop her. Already, she is not virgin. It will be no worse for her than it was for me. And she will like it better than I did. My place is with my man."

He was getting nowhere.

"All right, then," he said flatly. "I *am* married."

She sat up and stared at him. "Are you in love with her?"

He didn't answer. She wouldn't let him make it easy for her.

"In a church?" Trini demanded. "In a church, by a priest?"

"No! Goddamn it, I gave her father a horse and a rifle and some other junk. She's Indian."

"Indian!" Trini made a sound of derision. "That does not count! Myself, I am Spanish."

Spanish! If she had a drop of Spanish blood in her veins, he didn't know an Indian from a striped-ass ape!

"What kind of Spanish?" he asked sarcastically. "Yaqui Spanish? Tarahumara Spanish?"

"I am better than your Indian slut!" she flared. "Would she live in a cave like coyotes, with a bag of old *tortillas*? Or hide with you in a hole in Ramos' goat pen?"

"She'd have died for me! And I'll never see her again." He pushed Trini away and stood up.

Trini jumped up and pulled the arm around her neck and hugged it. "You don't have to love me. Let me be your woman. Not married, just your woman. I will die for you, too!"

"Oh, Trini . . ." he said, and found nothing to add, neither rejection nor reassurance. He looked out beyond the opening and the talus slope, not paying attention to what his eyes were telling him about the mesa top. He put his hand on her head.

Suddenly he hugged hard, squeezing her face against his chest. She struggled and pulled at his arm and mumbled.

"Shut up!" he hissed. "There's a rider out there!"

Chapter 14

THE HORSEMAN was not Lázaro and not Chuy, but almost certainly one of their men. Goatherds and shepherds did not wear big, swoop-brimmed hats, nor ride horses that moved with grace. This man rode with a lazy alertness, studying the ground.

Matt slid around the boulder to keep the rider in view. When the man came to the old sheep trail, he looked for tracks. He rode to the dried-up spring and looked around, and in a few minutes was gone down the sheep trail.

The whites of Trini's eyes gleamed in the dusk of the cave. Matt said, "I don't think he saw anything. If he did, he didn't give himself away."

Trini said, "We'd better go. I'll pick up the things."

"No, not yet. Let's think a minute. Most likely they've trailed us to the rock slide, and maybe the mule's tracks going away down the hill would lead them off. See what I mean? They would figure there was a rider, and get the idea planted in their heads, and not notice he was not ridden when he left the slide."

Trini watched him, big-eyed, and said again, "We'd better go to Ramos. He will hide us."

"Trini, keep quiet a minute! And I'm certain we left no track up to here. Only you can't ever be certain. Wo Ista used to see things on a trail that I did not notice."

"Is that her name?" Trini asked. "It is a stupid name!"

She sat and waited patiently. Matt stood a long time in thought. Finally he said, "If they have read those mule tracks, they will find us. It may take them a while, two or three days. Ramos may be in bad trouble, because it was his mule, and his place we started from. Unless he convinced them we stole the mule. He wouldn't be caught without a good story. Do you understand?"

"I understand," she said. "We will go to Ramos."

"No, I'm no good with this arm, and I don't think I could keep up. I'll risk it that they haven't smelled us out. Tell Ramos to get me a horse, any kind of a horse."

"You come, too, Mateo. Come now!"

He ignored her pleading look and took two gold coins from his pocket, the only two he had picked up when the bay bucked him off in Cocatlán.

"One of these is for Ramos, for the horse. You take the other, Trini. Go to Santa Fe, or somewhere. Travel only at night until you get across the border, and keep going." He handed her the coins.

"I'll get horses somewhere," she said, "and come back for you."

"Don't be a fool," Matt said, "just send me a horse by
Ramos. Get away while you can. The way I'll ride, you
couldn't keep up with me, anyway."

She began to cry.

Matt couldn't look at her. He said, "Hand me the shotgun."

When she handed it to him, he withdrew the ramrod
from its holders and probed the left barrel, the one with
the unbroken hammer. It was not loaded. He laid the shotgun down.

"Get me the revolver cylinder and the little package of
powder and shot from my jacket pocket," he ordered. He
had meant to use only a primer cap stored in the cylinder,
but suddenly realized the six pistol balls would make a
much more lethal load than the birdshot Ramos had sup-
plied.

She held out the cylinder and he said, "Hold it steady."

He pulled the knife out and pried the .36 caliber slugs out
of the chambers.

"Turn the cylinder over, Trini. Pour the powder into your
hand." She poured a small mound of black powder into
her palm.

"Now pour it down here." He picked up the shotgun and
leaned it against his thigh, muzzles up.

Trini began to pour in the powder.

"Stop! That one's no good, the hammer's broken. Pour it
all into the other barrel, the left one."

When she had poured the powder, he dropped the six
pistol balls in.

"Find me a rag, Trini, a piece of the petticoat."

She picked up a scrap of rag and flapped the dirt out of it
and gave it to him. He stuffed it into the barrel and rammed
it down onto the pistol balls with the ramrod.

"Now take the cotton out of the hole that runs through
the revolver cylinder and give me—"

She made a swift motion with her hand and hunkered
down, crouching. He looked where she indicated, out between the boulders, and drew a sharp breath.

A rider had come out of the junipers. He rode slowly,
reining his horse back and forth as he leaned to study the
ground.

"Lázaro!" Trini whispered.

Matt touched her shoulder. She turned to him. Her mouth
quivered.

"The percussion caps, inside the cylinder!" he whispered.

He pushed the knife at her. She pried the cotton out of the cylinder. Two of the caps fell out, and she scrabbled in the dirt for them.

Matt picked one up, placed it on the left nipple of the shotgun and pushed it down tight with his thumb.

"Lie down, Trini, as far back as you can get!" His whisper was harsh.

She scrambled on hands and knees to the back of the shelter and lay down. Matt slid to the opening and peered around the shoulder of the big boulder.

Lázaro was on the gray horse. His face was bandaged. He rode across the mesa to the dry spring, dismounted, and made an unhurried examination of the ground. Presently he straightened up and looked back along the face of the hill.

"Has he gone?" Trini asked anxiously.

He turned and scowled at her and shook his head, and turned again to watch Lázaro.

The Yaqui lifted his huge bulk into the saddle with grace and reined the horse around. He rode straight for the slide and the boulders behind which Matt crouched and Trini lay. He kept his fat face raised and his gaze on the opening.

Matt went swiftly to the back of the shelter and stretched out in front of Trini. He shifted his elbows until they were in position, and raised the shotgun. When he curled his right hand around the stock and poked his index and middle fingers around the two triggers, a flash of pain traveled up his right arm. He began to worry about what that tremendous charge—six powder loads for a pistol and six .36 caliber pistol balls—would do to the old damascus-twist barrel and the split stock, if he had to pull the trigger. His fingers around the triggers felt fat and useless. He didn't know which trigger fired the left barrel, but if Lázaro stuck his head around that rock he would pull them both, if his hand fell off!

He heard Lázaro climbing up to the boulders, not up the slide, but boldly up the easier slope beside it.

Lázaro's voice—the bad Spanish—came from around the boulder, just out of sight.

"Hello, *gringo*! Hello, *puta*!"

Matt held his breath. Trini gasped and gripped his ankle. Lázaro said, "You might as well come out. Old Man

Ramos wouldn't talk even when the rawhide had his eyes bulging. But there were suspicious marks. If there are tracks, my men will see them. So come out, or I will come in."

Trini whimpered. Lázaro began to laugh.

"Come in, then, big gut with a big mouth at one end!" Matt said, and tightened the slack out of the triggers, and scarcely felt the pain in hand and arm.

"Oh, an invitation, eh?" Lázaro laughed again. "Your house is mine, eh, as the saying goes? You are too anxious, *gringo*! What do you have in your hand, that Indian knife, perhaps? No, you had better come out to Lázaro."

"Are you going to take us to Chuy?" Trini asked. Her voice had the beginning of hysteria.

"Oh, no, whore! Chuy waits in Cocatlán for me to bring you. But Chuy will not have the pleasure. Not since your pimp, there, hit me and you threw the lamp at me and cut my face with the knife! When I am through with you and you can no longer squall for mercy, I will cave in a cutbank on you and tell Chuy you escaped."

He began snarling—"So, come out, slut! And you, cock with the broken wing! I lose patience, and it will be worse!"

Matt ran his tongue over his dry lips and said, "Lázaro, with the fifty meters of guts in his hog's body and a piece of gut for brain, still lacks the guts to come in. Against a frightened girl and a *gringo* with a broken arm."

There was an incoherent snarl outside, and Lázaro's bulk blotted out part of the opening.

Matt jerked both triggers.

The shotgun smashed against his shoulder. There was an unbearable blast of sound. Concussion pounded his ears.

Lázaro screamed, high and long-drawn, and the opening was a fog of smoke.

Matt writhed, clutching the broken wrist. He bit his lower lip, and felt as though his arm had been torn off at the elbow.

Through the roaring in his ears he began to hear a bubbling moan that rose to a shriek and trailed off to silence and rose again. He stumbled to the opening and looked down.

Lázaro lay jerking at the bottom of the slide, among the small boulders. His right shoulder was a great smear of blood, and the big arm flopped weirdly as he writhed.

Matt leaned against the boulder and surrendered for a

moment to the rhythmic spasms of agony. Lázaro still screamed, the sound swelling and receding.

Matt shook his head and called to Trini, "For God's sake, go down and shut him up! We've got to get out of here!"

He crawled in under the boulders and lay down. Trini picked up the shotgun and went out.

Presently Matt sat up. The screaming had stopped.

He got up and picked up the water bag and slung its thong around his neck. Slowly he clambered down the slope.

Trini was leading the gray horse from where it had trotted and then stopped to graze. Matt waited for her to bring it to him. He looked at Lázaro, that vast lump of bloody meat with a jagged splinter of bone showing white against the blood.

Lázaro's head was spiked to the ground, with half the length of the ramrod from the shotgun standing straight up from one ear. The shotgun leaned on his body, with the damascus-twist steel at the breech of the left barrel opened out like an unlaid rope.

"Is he quiet enough to suit you?" Trini asked.

Matt said, "Help me onto the horse. Is there a rifle in the boot?"

"Yes."

Trini made a step with her laced fingers, then straightened up. "Mateo," she said, "didn't you hear it? Somebody yelled."

Matt listened. His ears were still buzzing. "Are you sure? I can't hear anything. That rider that came before Lázaro must have heard the shot. Get back up to the rocks—we can't get away riding double . . ."

"It is too late."

Trini pointed to where the sheep track started down. Three riders partly screened by brush sat there motionless.

"Lie down!" Matt ordered. "Quick! That shot drew them like flies to rotting meat!"

He dropped to the ground and Trini crawled over to lie beside him, still holding the rein of the gray horse.

"Maybe they haven't seen us," Matt said. "They don't know just where the shot came from. Pull the horse over and get the rifle."

An idea came to him, a gamble without much chance to succeed, but better than lying there trying to fight off three gunmen.

"Give me the rein," he said, and when he had the rein

in his hand, "Get me Lázaro's jacket and *sombrero*. Crawl over, don't stand up!"

He looked toward the sheep track and the three men were in plain sight. One raised his arm and pointed, and they began to come on at a slow, wary walk.

Trini tugged and swore and pushed at Lázaro's body with her feet, and got the jacket off. The *sombrero* was a few yards away, and she crawled to it, dragging the bloody, torn jacket, and came scrambling back to Matt with them. The horse snorted and shied at the smell of blood, and Matt clung desperately to the rein until it quieted. He stood up, with the horse between him and the approaching horsemen, and said, "Help me put the jacket on. Just my left arm in the sleeve, then put it around my shoulders."

Blood soaked the jacket around the rips from the pistol slugs. He put on the *sombrero*. The shoulder seam of the jacket, the left one, hung halfway down his upper arm, and the jacket skirt halfway to his knees, in billows and folds.

He said, "There is a chance they can't see what's going on, from that distance, and I think they will obey Lázaro without question. Lie flat and have the rifle ready for me. If I cannot fool them, I will have to fight, right here."

He leaned against the gray horse on the near side, then drew a deep breath and yelled, "Hey-y-y!" as loud as he could.

Matt moved out partially in front of the horse, but still partly hidden, so the men would be sure to see the movement of his arm and recognize the jacket and *sombrero*.

It won't work! They'll never take me for him! But maybe, at this distance, and expecting to see Lázaro . . .

He swung his arm in the "Hurry up! That way!" signal, and yelled "*Pa' 'lla! Pa' 'lla!* Over there! Over there!"

The three riders spurred their mounts, took a course angling away in the direction he had pointed, and pounded away. They went into the scrub timber, out of sight, near where they had first come out.

Matt struggled out of the jacket and kicked it away. He dropped the *sombrero*, caught the saddle horn with his left hand and leaned his head on his arm and slumped against the horse.

Trini stood up holding the rifle, a Spencer carbine.

Without looking up, Matt said, "See if you can find his pistol. Here, I'll take the rifle."

She climbed slowly, searching among the rocks and gravel of the slide. Matt walked to Lázaro's body and unbuckled the bandolier of carbine cartridges and had to jerk hard to pull it from under the monstrosity of dead flesh. He rebuckled it and put it over his shoulder. He could not pull the pistol belt free, but managed to keep his fingers away from the congealing blood and got a dozen .44 cartridges from the loops.

Trini called, "Here it is!" and started back down to him. As she passed Lázaro's body, she spat on it. She handed Matt the revolver, and he put it in his waist band. Matt took the saddle and Trini got on behind.

"You carry the rifle," he said. "Have it ready if I need it. Those fellows will be back. We'll go down the sheep track."

"No!" Trini objected. "It comes out at the road, less than a kilometer from Cocatlán!"

"Doesn't matter," Matt said. "We're not going to follow those three riders."

He lifted the rein. Trini thumped her heels on the gray's ribs. It began to canter.

They had gone a kilometer down the trail, and Matt's hearing was returning to normal. He could hear no sound of pursuit.

He began to watch for a way to get off the sheep trail, some place that would not show horse tracks, and presently saw it—an outcropping of flat rock that crossed the rough trail. He turned the horse up hill.

Trini said sharply, "Mateo, wake up! We are off the trail!"

"We have to rest this horse. He brought that lard of a Lázaro up the mountain already today and now, riding double like this, we must go easy on him."

He found a place behind a big boulder. Trini helped him down. His right arm throbbed steadily with every thrust of his pulse.

Trini stripped the saddle from the gray. She staggered under its weight and that of the carbine in its scabbard. She took off the ornate bridle with its silver-mounted chino bit and tied the horse to a shrub with the *mecate*.

Matt laid Lázaro's .44 on the ground behind the boulder and stretched out beside it. Trini came to lie at his side. She took his left hand and laid it against her cheek.

"Well, we are still alive," she said, "and Lázaro, the hog, is dead, and screaming in the fires of hell. Let's start north.

When it is dark enough, we can go down to the road."

"We have to have another horse, Trini. The gray cannot carry double forever, and it we have to run . . . We must get food, somewhere, and more water. How far are we from the road to Cocatlán?"

"It is a matter of a few kilometers only—" She stopped in mid-sentence. "Mateo, you are not thinking—you will not . . . ?"

"I am going to get my horse."

"Oh, Mateo! Chuy nearly killed you there in the *cantina*. We are lucky to be alive. And your arm—you could not fight—" She drew a shuddering breath. "Please, Mateo! Let's just go north. It is only a few nights of travel and, in your own country . . ."

"Trini, I came for that horse, and I am going to take him back!"

Suddenly she cried, "Is that the horse that bought your Indian slut, that she-fox-in-heat? Is she the one that made that sheath for your knife, that ugly thing with the beads that nearly got you killed when Lázaro recognized it? Go then! Go and get yourself killed. I hope you do! You and the horse, too! And I hope she is dead, that Indian whore!"

She stamped away and began to cry.

Matt picked up Lázaro's saddle and slung it one-handed onto the horse's back. He hung the bandolier of cartridges on the horn and picked up the revolver. He untied the *mecate* and wadded it together and managed to tie it with a saddle string. His mounting was clumsy and painful.

Trini brought the water bag and looped its thong over the saddle horn. She was still sniffling, but she said, "I am coming."

"No!" Matt said. "Go to Ramos' place. If I do not come by tomorrow night, then start north. Go to my cousin, Paco Gómez, at my ranch near Ojo Prieto and tell him what happened. Tell him I said you can stay there until you decide what to do. They will help you."

But she climbed up behind him and said, "I will go with you. I am your woman!"

Chapter 15

IT WAS three hours past sunset, and black dark, and they had come down the mountain and across the *chaparral*-choked flat. Cocatlán lay just ahead.

Matt stopped the gray in the brush, a hundred yards from the archway. Stars were brilliant and there was a glow in the east—there would be a moon.

He said, "Get down, Trini, so I can get off. Then mount again, and get the rifle. If you shoot it, then just pull the lever and push it back, and another cartridge is ready. If Pecas is there and if I am lucky, there will be no trouble. But if you hear shouting or any gunfire, ride to the arch and wait until I come."

Trini dismounted and helped him down. He said ~~member~~, stay right here. If anything happens, ride to the arch, no farther!"

She pulled his head down and kissed him, and her cheeks were wet.

At the arch, he leaned against the crumbling bricks and looked back. He could see the silhouette of Trini on the horse, crouched over the horn trying to watch him. Some projection of her fear reached him, and tension began to build in him until his chest felt tight. He looked cautiously through the arch.

Lamps spread yellow fans of light on the cobblestones. He caught the musty smell of wet, burned wood, and saw the shape of crazily tilted rafters thrusting up, naked of tiles. That must be the burned-out *cantina*, the Palomar.

Nearer, the Cantina Bugambilia was noisy. Three men went in. A down-running succession of guitar chords sounded rich and silvery above laughter. Matt slipped around the arch and began to walk slowly up the street. From a dark doorway, a voice said, right at his shoulder, *"Buena noche!"* Everything inside of him jumped, but he walked on and murmured over his shoulder, *"Buena noche, amigo!"*

There were horses at the hitchrack in front of the

Bugambilia. The nearest one shifted and, momentarily, lamplight splashed across its spotted rump.

Matt crossed the street, angling across to the other wall of house fronts. When he was halfway across, a horse walked through the arch behind him, at the end of the street. He controlled the compulsion to run, and continued to walk slowly until he had got across and leaned against a wall. The horseman stopped, somewhere behind him. Matt walked on, keeping close to the wall.

He stopped opposite the horses at the hitchrack, just out of the light spilling from the doorway of the *cantina*. He looked at Pecas, the Appaloosa stallion from the Palouse country of Idaho, two thousand miles north and a thousand miles west of Cocatlán.

For a moment there was no Cocatlán and no Chuy, no Mexican whore waiting for him outside an archway, no sweat in the palms of his hands, and no ache in his arm. Just a small, spotted stallion with a split ear, standing slant-hipped in lamp light. Matt whispered, "Hello, horse," and did not realize that he had whispered in Cheyenne.

He tried to see into the shadows, up and down the street. Two women were jabbering to each other from opposite doorways farther along. Two cigarettes glowed and dimmed and glowed again beside a doorway three houses up from the *cantina*, where two lumps of shadow might be neighbors with their chairs tilted against the wall. Matt walked across to the horse.

On its off side, he felt the smooth texture of a leather saddle scabbard and the butt of a carbine protruding from it. Pecas swung his head and nickered. Matt crouched and drew the pistol and squeezed the trigger and thumbed back the hammer at the same time, so there would be no click as he cocked it. He bent his head down behind Pecas' shoulder and held his breath.

Chuy came and stood in the doorway and saw him.

Matt held the cocked revolver under the skirt of his jacket and stumbled away down the street, singing, ". . . *en esta noche, la quiero olvidar* . . ." off key, and wondering if he was overdoing it.

He broke off the song and yelled back over his shoulder, "Goddamn horse—wassamatter keep horses in a street—man can't walk home . . . bump into some horse's ass . . ." He began to sing again.

Behind him Chuy laughed and went back into the *cantina*.
Matt leaned against the wall of a house and felt the hammering pulse beating at his bad arm. He straightened up and went quickly back to the hitchrack and pushed in between Pecas and the next horse. He shoved the revolver into his waistband, swiftly drew the skinning knife and cut the reins. The horse at his back shifted nervously, but Pecas stood quiet.

Chuy came to the door and peered suspiciously toward him. Suddenly he yelled, "The *gringo!*" and ran at Matt.

The stirrup hung high for Matt, but he got his foot in it and swung up and squeezed with his left knee. Pecas spun and began to trot down the street. Matt crouched over the saddle horn, expecting the shot. He needed no rein for the Appaloosa—his hand was free to draw the cocked pistol. He had just got it clear when the shot came and the uproar broke loose, the yelling and cursing and another shot, and a raking burn across his shoulder like the sear of a branding iron.

He could not swing far enough around to aim, but he let go three shots and heard one buzz off the cobblestones. The stallion was galloping now, and a rifle joined in behind him, its blasting explosions almost deafening in the confinement of the two rows of houses. Matt pushed with his knee, and Pecas swerved and ran along house walls, so close that Matt's knee bumped a door frame. Someone made a flying dive into a dark doorway.

Almost at the arch, a mounted figure burst from the shadow of a wall and hurtled toward him. Cursing, Matt swung the pistol and fired, too high and too wide.

The figure yelled, "Mateo! I am Trini! I am Trini!"

Pecas went pounding through under the arch, and the gray horse, with Trini still yelling on its back, plunged through behind. Instantly, Matt grabbed a handful of mane with his pistol hand and pulled. The stallion squatted almost on its buttocks and slid to a halt. Trini's gray went hammering past, and Matt yelled at her to come back. She made the gray circle, and came back to him at a trot.

"What's the matter?" she shrilled. "Are you hurt? Is the horse shot? Hurry! Get up behind!"

"Get down!" Matt demanded. "Quick! Bring the rifle!"

"You are crazy! They are coming!"

She started to turn the gray, and Matt yelled, "Bring that

rifle! Get down, and don't let the horse get away!"

She slid down and brought the carbine. Matt seized the rein of the gray horse and said, "Start shooting, up the street!"

"I don't know how!"

"Damn it, start shooting! Just pull the trigger!"

The carbine in her hands roared and spouted orange flame, and the bullet went off somewhere in the sky. The gray horse plunged, but Matt held it.

"Keep on, Trini! Pull the lever back and . . ."

Trini remembered.

She began to pour shots up the street, and the trample of approaching hoofs became a confusion and a retreat. There was yelling and swearing up by the Bugambilia, and a few shots. Chips of brick stung Matt's face, and a horse shrieked in pain. Then the street was silent.

Trini ran to the gray and scrambled up.

"Wait, Trini! In a minute we go!"

Matt dismounted and led the stallion to the arch and stopped him under it. He got the carbine from Chuy's saddle boot, clamped it under his right arm and pulled the lever back and got a shell into the chamber.

He turned Pecas broadside across the street and told him in Cheyenne to stand. He laid the carbine across the saddle and put the butt against his left shoulder. He took up the slack of the trigger with his forefinger and lined the sights on the lamplit door of the *cantina*.

Trini began to whimper and said, "For the love of God . . ."

"Shut up!" he snarled.

Then a wide hat appeared in the doorway, the barrel of a rifle showed underneath it. Matt's shot knocked chips from the doorframe. The head jerked back so fast the hat fell off.

"All right," Matt said, "now we go. But walk your horse so there is no sound of galloping to tell them we have gone. It will be a few minutes before anyone comes into the street, now."

He put the carbine into the boot and mounted. He was getting quite adept at mounting one-handed. There was no need to shorten reins and grab a handful of mane with Pecas.

After five minutes he said, "All right, Trini! Push that horse!"

He let Pecas run and, for two miles, did not slow him except to let Trini catch up. The gray was beginning to blow when Matt ordered, "Turn off here. There is no use trying to hide our tracks, yet. You lead, now, and take us into the foothills as directly as you can. When we get into the canyons we will find a way to lose them."

Wordlessly she turned the gray off the road. Matt urged the stallion alongside. "First," he said, "what were you doing on the street? If I were a better shot with a pistol, you would be dead. I told you to wait in the field."

Trini turned her face toward him. "Regina," she said. "I thought perhaps I could see her once more. Our house is the third inside the arch. I thought maybe, even, I could take her with us."

"Well . . ." Matt began.

"I saw her," Trini said. "I got down from the horse and looked through the window, where the shutter is broken. That young *vaquero*, the one who wanted to marry me, he was there and he was drunk, but Regina was drunker."

Matt's anger died abruptly. He could think of nothing to say about Regina.

"Lead off, Trini, and push the horse all he will stand. As soon as there's enough light, I've got to do something about this shoulder."

"Mateo! You were hit!" She jerked the horse to a stop.

"Go on, Trini! It is only a gouge. That *hideputa* can shoot, even in the dark!"

For a while they struck straight across country, and the going was bad. The great patches of *nopal*, the *mesquite,* the *tornillo*, looked feathery in the moonlight, but hooked viciously with their assortment of claws and barbs; the small *arroyos* were hard to see, and the gray horse stumbled often. Then Trini found a cart track which meandered but kept a general course for the loom of the hills. Once they heard distant shouts and the drumming of hoofs, far back on the road.

"Is there any water in the bag?" Matt asked.

"A couple of liters, no more," Trini said.

"Pull up, then. Hold it so I can cut the top off," Matt ordered. "That gray horse must have water."

He cut the top from the goat skin, and the gray sniffed

at the bag while Trini held it, did not like the smell, and turned its head. Then it changed its mind and sucked up the water, all there was left.

"Well, there's only one thing to do," Matt said. "Go to Ramos' place. There ought to be water there, and maybe something to eat. We'll kill a goat if we have to."

"Mateo, we cannot go there! Ramos is dead!"

"Ramos dead! What do you mean?"

"Lázaro said he would not talk when they tortured him, remember?"

"I didn't hear him, or I've forgotten," Matt said. "But that doesn't have to mean he's dead!"

"You are a fool," Trini said. "Of course it does, whether he talked or not."

"It's the only place we can get water and food," Matt insisted. "We can travel the hundred kilometers to the border in three nights. Can you find it without using the road?"

"Yes, I'll find it." Trini thumped her heels on the gray's ribs and reined it off the cart track.

Matt's shoulder, where Chuy's bullet had plowed across the trapezius, was sore and hot.

As they passed below the mesa where Lázaro lay, Matt saw that she was trying to choose a way that would leave as little sign of their passing as she could contrive. Once during the night they stopped to rest. Nearly stupid with exhaustion himself, he marveled at the toughness of the slight girl. She was so tired she staggered when she dismounted to tighten the cinch. She remounted with great effort.

"Trini," he said gently, "you have been fine, very brave, and you have not complained. I know how much you have done for me."

He pulled jacket and *camisa* away from his shoulder. The pulling loose of the *camisa*, glued to the wound with dry blood, made him cry out.

Trini exclaimed in sympathy, and rode close.

"Nothing we can do now, Trini," he said. "Maybe Ramos has salve or grease. We will wash it and find something for a bandage." His face was flushed and hot, and the ache was back at the base of his skull as it had been when his broken arm was swollen from the splint bindings. The arm did not ache so much now, and the swelling was down. They rode on toward Ramos' shack.

Just after daylight, they dismounted up the hill from the

shack. Matt took the revolver and told Trini to stay hidden and make no noise, and went carefully through the brush. Four buzzards launched themselves clumsily and flew away. The goats and the mule were gone.

Ramos was stretched on his back with his hands and feet tied to stakes with rawhide, which had doubtless been put on wet, and had pulled taut in drying. There was a rawhide thong around his head.

Matt kept his eyes averted and went into the shack. He found a few dry ears of corn and a little meal in a small iron kettle. In a corner was a small jar stoppered with a corn cob. He took out the stopper and sniffed. There was *tequila* in the jar.

That was all he found. There was no water in the barrel behind the shack. He put the jar in the kettle with the corn and the meal and went back to Trini.

She said, "He's dead, isn't he!" She was crying silently. "Can we bury him, Mateo? At least that much for him?"

"No, Trini. If his body is moved, Chuy will know we have been here. We must go right now! There is no water. We must find water before night or the horses will give out, and without horses we are finished. We must have it for ourselves, too."

He handed her the kettle. She tied it to a saddle string, where it swung and bumped the shoulder of the gray horse as he began to walk.

Chapter 16

SLOWLY THEY made their way north, keeping in the scrub timber of the foothills. Matt's tongue swelled and he did not know whether it was fever in his wound or thirst that plagued him most. Trini was in equal difficulty—he knew from the way she swayed in the saddle and from her painful attempts to swallow. The gray horse began stumbling.

They caught glimpses of the road which they were trying to parallel. Scarcely anything moved on it. There was an occasional ox-cart and several burro trains, but nothing that might be considered a patrol sent out by Chuy to scour the road. If he was not on the road, he must be following, picking out the trail. When was he going to strike? Matt listened for sounds of pursuit—the distant shout, the sound of horses. His thirst and the fever of his infected wound were mounting, his ears were ringing, and he could not hear well.

The gray horse stumbled and went to its knees, and Trini pitched off over its head. The meal kettle spilled its contents, and the *tequila* jar rolled along the ground and came to rest.

The gray struggled to its feet, but Trini did not get up. Matt dismounted and went to her. She looked up at him and tried to speak, but could not. Matt could see her swollen tongue between cracked lips. He got the *tequila* jar and, clamping it between his knees, pulled the stopper.

Trini sat up and drank a little of the *tequila* and handed it back to him. The jar hurt his cracked lips, and the liquor was fiery on his tongue. He took a long swallow and stoppered the jar.

"Can you ride?" His voice was raucous.

Trini croaked something and managed to mount. He put the jar in the kettle and picked up the ears of corn. The meal was scattered and he did not try to scoop it up. He had to try twice before he got the stirrup, and when he was in the saddle he thought, if I get down again before we find water, I won't be able to get back.

Much later, they rode out of the timber onto a shoulder of hill and gazed across a wide, dry valley at a steep declivity about two kilometers ahead. Matt saw birds flitting purposefully through the brush and watched them rise and fly across the valley until they were lost against the drabness of its coloring. Something leaped inside him, a thrill of excitement. He looked up into the clear turquoise of sky and saw flights of larger birds flying straight across the valley.

"Trini," he croaked, "if you see anything move, any animal, tell me."

She swallowed painfully and said, "There are jack rabbits, four or five."

Matt strained his burning eyes and saw them. They were not together, but all going the same way without pausing to browse.

"Come on," Matt said. "There's water over there somewhere."

In the last flare of sunset, he saw the telltale sign high on the hill, the patch of living green in the scorched drabness of brown *chaparral*.

As they reached the far side of the flat and started up the hill, Pecas whinnied and flared his dust-dry nostrils and began to climb powerfully. The gray lifted its slogging head and dug in its toes and almost kept up with the stallion.

Before dark, Matt and Trini lay beside a hollow they had scooped in the silt under a green young tree, and watched the clear water of the tiny spring filter in.

Matt's belly hurt from too much water. The horses had each had a swallow and, tied a few feet away, were cropping coarse grass. Presently, when the hole filled, Matt would bring them one at a time for more.

Matt said, "We will rest here tonight, and tomorrow, if Chuy does not come. In the morning I will show you how to get food. My head is sick now. Trini, will you wash this bullet slash, and then pour *tequila* on it?"

He stretched out face down and went to sleep while she washed the wound, and roused only at the bite of the *tequila* on the inflamed gouge.

During the night, he woke half-delirious, to find Trini bathing his hot temples. When he slept again, dream pictures flitted through his mind like a magic-lantern show—tall Cheyenne lodges sending up thin blue spirals of smoke, a vast herd of buffalo running like a brown sea over rolling prairie, the honeymoon lodge in the aspens and, many times, he called out to Wo Ista and joked with her and said the tender, courting words. And finally, there again was Wohk Pos Its falling from the spotted stallion with his spine shot away.

Matt groaned and sat up. Pearly light crept down the hill. Trini sat glowering at him, sulky because she had recognized Wo Ista's name in his mumbling. He tried to get up, but a chill compounded of dawn cold and his illness swept him. Trini came and put a horse blanket around his shoulders. She said, "Give me your knife. I will find a flint and strike a fire to boil the corn."

Matt's mind was barely clear enough to consider what she had said. "Dig a hole for the fire, so it will not be seen," he said.

When the fire was burning in the hole, Trini filled the kettle and gave Matt a drink. When she began to cut the kernels from the cobs, he said, "Save one ear. We will use it for bait in a snare. Maybe we can get a quail or two."

They shared the coarse mush. Afterward, at Matt's direction Trini plucked long hairs from the tail of the gray horse, knotted them together and made a running noose.

"Spread it under a bush," Matt said. "Prop it partly off the ground with a small stick and spread it open with a straw. Lead the end of the string to some bush where you can hide. Scatter a line of kernels leading to the noose. If a quail gets its head in the noose, pull quickly, then let him fight it."

Trini scraped the kernels from the corn cob, took the snare and went down the hill. Quail were converging on the spring, sending out their three-note rallying call.

Matt sat fidgeting at the burning of the wound on his shoulder. The swelling of his right wrist was much reduced. He flexed the fingers of his right hand, and there was little pain. He went to sleep.

When Trini woke him she had three quail, already skinned and gutted. She spitted them on sticks stuck in the ground around the fire hole. When they were cooked, Matt ate one. Trini gnawed at another and tried to make him take the third one, but he had no more appetite.

All afternoon, he rolled and muttered in semi-consciousness. At dusk, Trini woke him and held out a handful of something purple, a pulpy mass.

"Here, eat," she said. There were purple smears around her mouth.

"What is it?" Matt asked.

"*Tuna,* the fruit of *nopal* cactus. I scraped the thorns off."

Matt gagged on the bland pulp, but ate doggedly.

"I got *nopal* pads, too. I am boiling them for a poultice. It is very good for wounds. It draws out the poison. Now, turn over and lie face down. Here, first we will take off your *camisa.*"

She produced a rag, a strip of green cotton. She laughed. "From my last petticoat," she explained. "And it is clean. I boiled it before I put the *nopal* pads in the kettle."

When she had spread a steaming lump of the pulp on the rag and folded it over, she warned, "It must be very hot or it does no good. Be ready!"

The hot poultice on the wound was a blistering agony. Matt

cried out and writhed, but Trini got a knee between his shoulders and held him down and put pressure on the poultice with the knife blade. As the poultice began to cool some of the fire went out of the wound. He lay limp and was almost asleep when Trini slapped the second poultice in place. Matt yelled and humped his back. Trini sat astride him and swore at him and told him to lie still. When he lay quiet again, she said, "We will leave it tied in place. Now, eat again, and then sleep."

Throughout the night, the delirium came back. Trini wrapped both saddle blankets around him and huddled against him when the fever gave way to shuddering chills.

When morning came, he was out of his head. He slept all day as though dead, and toward evening, awoke clear-headed. Trini squatted by the firepit, the gaunt planes of her face underlit with the glow of coals. She smiled at him.

"I got four more quail." She speared a roasted bird with the knife and brought it to him. "Tonight we feast. I have sliced a big puffball for frying in the kettle, and I gathered a skirtful of juniper berries for the horses."

Matt was still ravenous when they had eaten all Trini had prepared. The fever had subsided in his shoulder and the headache was only a dull undercurrent of pain. He began to worry again.

"When you went down the hill, could you see any movement on our back trail? I cannot believe Chuy is so stupid he cannot follow our trail."

"I saw nothing, Mateo."

Matt said, "Maybe he has decided the horse is not worth all the trouble."

"Mateo, it is not the horse. The real thing is that you shamed him. He will never forget it. Maybe one of his men turned on him at last. He has many enemies. Or maybe he has gone on a smuggling trip."

"We dare not count on it," Matt said, "but we will risk traveling by day. We will leave in the morning."

"And when we are across the Río Bravo into your country, we will be safe."

"Trini . . ." Matt began. But there was no point in telling her. She had got it into her head that the Río Bravo, the Río Grande to Americans, was some magic line beyond which Chuy would not follow. But just to get there! To get rested and well! If, then, Chuy still kept after him, he would

have the odds his way, for once! But the border and the
ranch and Paco and Ana were still two nights away . . .

He walked over to look at Pecas, and was startled at the
weakness of his knees. He cursed Chuy when he saw the
half-healed spur slashes on the Appaloosa's flanks and the
saddle gall among the spots on its back. Pecas let himself
be hugged. He pushed hard with his forehead, rubbing it up
and down Matt's chest. Matt picked up the feet one by one to
look for sand cracks, but found none.

The gray horse was a good mount, well put up, gentle and
well trained. It, too, bore the marks of harsh usage, old saddle
galls and spur scars. It was alert and ready.

Trini came from behind nearby bushes, bare to the waist
and embarrassed. She wore only a petticoat, knee-length and
ragged where she had slashed it off to use for bandages.

She said, "Now that I am your woman, I have no modesty.
My clothes are filthy. I pounded up *yucca* root for soap."
She dropped the dirty, flounced skirt and the grimy blouse
into the kettle and began to slosh them up and down with a
stick. She kept her eyes lowered and would not look at him,
although she was obviously aware of his frank enjoyment of
the swell of full, small breasts and the near-black nipples
against copper-tan skin. He sat on a saddle blanket and
watched her.

She slapped the skirt and blouse against a rock to knock
the suds from them. When she had rinsed them and spread
them to dry, she came shyly and sat against Matt's side. Gently
she pushed him down and lay half across his chest and
kissed him. Matt untied the tabs and pushed the petticoat
down around her knees. She probably hadn't ever known that
some women wore underpants. He pushed her aside and stood
to shuck off *guaraches, calzones* and *camisa*. He felt strong
as a bull.

Ten minutes later, she lay panting. "You are a bull! What
wonders will you perform when you get your strength back!"

"I have it back," Matt laughed. "That is, I will have it back
in a little while. You are a better poultice than boiled cactus
pads!"

He lay a while utterly at peace, watching the sky change
from rose to lavender to blue-black as the sunset faded. His
arm was numb from Trini's weight. Chuy nagged at his
thoughts. No one could have failed to read that trail from
Cocatlán to here! Had he given up the stupidity of face

saving? Matt couldn't quite believe so—but maybe it had been only Lázaro to whom revenge was all important. Still, Matt had driven Chuy and his maniac pride out of the plaza at Ojo Prieto, had escaped from him at Cocatlán, and had taken back the horse. No, Chuy wouldn't quit! Well, think about it later. For now, take advantage of this puzzling respite Chuy was permitting, and concentrate on getting home.

He got up and said, "I might as well bathe while I'm naked as a jaybird." He filled the kettle and put in a handful of the pounded *yucca* root and set it on the coals.

He washed his head and front and legs. Trini said, "I'll do your back."

He stood and shivered while she sloshed the hot, soapy water over him with a rag. She traced the outline of the old horn scar under his shoulder blade with a gentle finger.

"What is this? Were you shot before?"

"No, a buffalo cow that I thought was dead, but wasn't. I turned my back."

"And who treated *this* one, Mateo? It is in a place you could not reach."

Matt knew what she was getting at. Why in hell doesn't she let it alone! he thought, and sudden anger made his voice harsh.

"My wife!" he said and watched her eyes go stony. "She took the cow's stomach and cut it open and put it on the wound, like your cactus poultice."

Trini dropped the rag and walked away, the set of her shoulders announcing her anger and jealousy. Abruptly, he wanted to hurt her, and called after her, "She was a wonderful wife. She was beautiful. She could skin a buffalo in fifteen minutes. She could ride better than you. She made beautiful clothing. She was virgin when I bought her, and I would not trade her for the fanciest Mexican whore that ever made her living on her back!"

Trini ran blindly down the hill. He heard her sobbing while he dressed and lay down and pulled the horse blankets around himself.

Late at night as he lay shivering Trini crawled in beside him and crept within the circle of his arm. She got his arm under her neck and put her head on his chest. His hand caressed her cheek. He began to talk, and one part of his mind was surprised and reluctant—how long had this impulse been there?

"We will be married, Trini, when we get back."

He heard the small gasp of her indrawn breath. She lay still as a frightened bird, and he felt the sudden accelerated beat of her heart against his ribs.

"We will build a house next to Paco and Ana. But there is one thing—we will never speak of Wo Ista. That is over and I will never see her again. We will have a bargain. I will never say anything to you about your life there in Cocatlán, I will not even think about it. And for your part, stop thinking about her. It just makes trouble."

"Tell me about her, Mateo, just once. Everything. Then I will stop wondering. I will still hate her, but I will not say it."

"I lived with her people, the Cheyenne, Trini, and it was a good life. I bought her from her father with a horse and other things. Her father gave the horse to her brother, who was my friend. Then I got tired of the life in the Indian camps and went back to buffalo hunting. Only a month ago, I was in a big camp with other hunters, a place like a small town, with three sod houses and a saloon and a blacksmith shop and store. We were breaking the law, hunting in a country that had been set aside for Indians. A great war party of Comanche and Cheyenne and Arapahoe attacked us and we fought them off for three days. In the fighting, Wo Ista's brother, Wohk Pos Its, was riding the stallion. I killed him. So, even if I wanted to, I could not go back to her. She loved me, but now she will hate me."

"How would she know it was you that shot him?" Trini asked.

"Indians miss nothing, Trini. They will know every hunter who was in the camp and what every man did in the battle, hunters and Indians both. Everything that every man did will be sung about in the lodges—how many bullets he fired, and who counted first coup and who second. Nothing will be forgotten. So you see why I could not go back. So you are not ever to speak of her again, and things will be right between us."

"I promise, Mateo. I will be a better wife than she was. And I am glad you have told me."

His arm was going to sleep, but he would not move it. After a while, Trini slept, and he tried gently to withdraw the arm, but she murmured and pressed close to him. He thought, what the hell have I done! He lay until daylight, half regretting and half glad that he had made the decision.

Quail began to call. Pecas snorted and shook himself. Trini awoke and smiled with sudden radiance. She kissed him and smoothed his hair and, finally, got off his numb arm.

Matt said, "We had better move. I don't like not knowing where Chuy is. Something is queer about this. Fill the *tequila* jar and the kettle, then help me saddle up."

Matt made sure that the two Spencer carbines and Lázaro's revolver were loaded. He felt good. There was hardly any swelling left in the broken arm, and he could use his right hand without too much pain. The fever was gone from his shoulder, and it was healing well.

Chapter 17

THE GOING was not too bad. They got high enough to be above most of the cactus and *yucca,* and there were open glades among the pine and juniper, with hardly any brush. Matt did not know how far south of the river they were, but they would get there just by traveling north.

At nightfall they stopped to rest. They shared the water in the *tequila* jar and gave the horses what was in the kettle. When they had eaten the remaining quail, they slept while the horses grazed around their picket stakes. Stars indicated about two A.M. when they started north again. Toward morning the hills began to flatten, and once more they rode among *chaparral* and cactus. Just before daylight, they came to the river. They pushed their way through a tangle of low willows and the horses stood fetlock deep in mud among tule reeds and sucked up the silted brown water.

Matt and Trini got down and drank. Trini said, "The Río Bravo! And the other bank is New Mexico and we are safe! For a while, when you were so sick, I thought we could not do it."

Matt wiped his wet mouth and stood up and got a foot in the stirrup. "Trini," he said, "I had better tell you. We are not safe. We are in more danger right now than any time since I got the horse back."

"But, Mateo, there has been no sign of Chuy, and we are so close now. Just across the river."

"That's the trouble, Trini. And that's why we have not seen him. He is not stupid. Why should he trail us through rough country when he knew where I would go? He will be waiting for us, probably at the ford."

Trini rose hastily. Her panic showed in her eyes as she mounted the gray.

"Now wait!" Matt said sharply. "We are not going to let him trap us! We won't take the ford, we'll keep going downstream. I'll remember landmarks and know where we are. We'll turn away from the river before we get to the ford, and go through the brush and keep away from the road. And if he comes to the ranch, I will have the big buffalo gun, and that will be a different matter."

Matt kicked Pecas' ribs and the stallion turned downstream, stirring clouds of mud in the slow current.

"We'll stay in the river as much as we can," Matt said, "even though no one is following. Make the gray horse stay behind Pecas."

At a wide bend, a jut-hipped longhorn bull challenged them and threw sand over its back. Deer fled from the river as they approached and on a mud bank were the flower-like footprints of a jaguar. A band of javelina scattered and left their musky stink hanging in the hot air. About nine o'clock, Matt began to recognize half-remembered places where, as children, he and Paco had swum and hunted—the place where they had shot the big buck, and a backwater where he had got seven sitting mallards with one blast of his father's shotgun.

"Come on, Trini, let's get out of the river. We'll take to the brush."

And as he turned Pecas, there was a spout of water under the stallion's nose, and the crash of a rifle-shot from the brush on the far bank, and Chuy's voice yelling, "Not the horse, damn you! Shoot the Goddamned *gringo!*"

Pecas leaped sideways and Trini screamed, and Matt almost went into the river. He got hold of the saddle horn. The gray horse went past him, plunging, throwing sheets of water, with Trini hunched over and clinging to its neck.

The rifle—two rifles!—crashed out again. The gray horse

stumbled, regained its footing and scrambled up the bank.

Matt hooked his right knee around the cantle of the saddle and swung down as far as he could, side-riding the Appaloosa. It smashed its way through the water, came out of it and was up the bank and into the willows, surefooted as a buffalo.

Back across the river, Chuy was cursing, his voice high-pitched as he screamed orders to bring horses. He fired five times with the revolver, and the slugs clipped twigs and leaves.

Pecas burst out of the brush. Beyond lay bare ground, gullies and washes, heaps of scoured boulders and, half a mile away, a low butte with sloping, eroded sides.

Ahead, the gray horse struggled up the side of a wash, with Trini kicking its ribs.

The road was somewhere off to the right. Pecas, running hard, swung to follow the gray, the great bellows of his ribs pumping under Matt's gripping calves, and the powerful quarters driving him in a tearing gallop. Matt looked back, but nothing showed yet in the wall of brush that bordered the river. When he looked ahead again, he saw a splash of blood on the ground.

Oh, Jesus! She's hit!

The stallion took the slope of the wash in three plunging leaps and went over the lip. Ahead, close now, the gray was trotting. Matt jerked the stallion's mane, and it slowed its headlong rush and caught up with the gray.

"Are you hit?" Matt shouted.

"No, but there's something wrong with the horse. He won't run!"

The gray's head swung low, and there was a froth of blood at its lips.

Matt said, "He's done for. Make him keep up if you can."

He pushed the stallion ahead of the gray, and it began to canter. He kneed it over to the right, to head for the road.

Trini called, "Mateo! I can't keep up!"

The gray was cantering drunkenly. Past Trini and the horse, over the lip of the wash, Matt saw three riders come out of the brush.

Matt rode back and caught the rein of the gray.

"Beat him, Trini! Kick him! I'll pull!"

There was a shout behind. Matt kicked Pecas and was almost pulled from the saddle as the stallion leaped ahead.

The gray galloped a little faster. Matt swung his head, searching for some place to make a stand, and saw the low *mesa* over to the left.

He stopped the stallion. The gray stopped and stood with forelegs spread and head hanging. The blood from its mouth was a thin stream.

Matt dismounted and got the Spencer carbine from the saddle boot.

"Get down, Trini! Hurry!"

She dismounted quickly.

Matt ordered, "Get on the stallion. Ride to the road, straight that way!" He pointed. "Then turn left. When you come to a plank bridge, that is my place. Tell Paco—"

"Mateo! Get up behind me!" She was in the saddle now, very scared, looking back.

"I'll climb up the *mesa* and hold them off. Tell Paco—"

Trini was crying now. "No, Mateo! I won't leave you!" She swung her leg back across the cantle.

Matt hit her.

"Shut up! Gallop the horse all the way! Tell Paco to bring me the big buffalo gun! And the bag of cartridges! Tell him to ride up onto the far end of the *mesa* there, and tie the stallion, then sneak down to this end with the gun. I'll be up above here somewhere. I need that gun!"

They could hear the horses galloping now, out of sight over the rim of the wash.

"I'm not going! I'm going to—"

Matt slapped the stallion hard on its spotted rump, and it ran, going full gallop with the first jump. Trini lost both of the too-long stirrups, but clung to the horn.

Matt watched, fearing that she would try to circle and come back, but she leaned over and slapped the stallion's neck. It swung around a cutbank and was out of sight.

Matt jammed the Spencer carbine into the saddle scabbard on the gray, alongside the other carbine. He mounted and turned the stumbling horse up a shallow *arroyo* that led up the side of the *mesa*. It trotted twenty steps and went to its knees. Matt got off fast and jerked the two carbines from the scabbard, afraid the horse would fall on them. The gray struggled to its feet, but its head drooped. Matt laid the carbines down and drew the .44 and shot it between the eyes. It fell heavily.

Matt got the carbines under his arm. He began to climb.

Faintly, he could hear running hoof-beats in the direction Trini had gone. She found the road, he thought, and stopped to listen. There was no sound of horses approaching up the *arroyo,* and he concluded that Chuy had heard the pistol shot and stopped.

The *arroyo* narrowed and petered out. Matt looked past the wash to the thickets by the river. There was no movement. They're in that wash, wondering about the shot, he thought, and began to climb again.

Nothing happened while he made his way up to the rim of the *mesa.* He found a heap of rocks on the edge, where he could see all around and could check behind him. He knew the carbines were loaded, but he examined them again, seven cartridges in the tubular magazine in each gun butt, and one in each chamber. There were fourteen more .52 caliber cartridges for the carbines, in the bandolier he had pulled from Lázaro's bloody hulk, and a dozen in his jacket pocket for the revolver. He punched out the expended shell in the revolver and loaded that chamber and the empty one on which the hammer had rested.

He lay and sweated and watched and listened for what seemed a long time before anything happened. Then the head of a horse and the head and torso of a rider showed at the top of the wash. It was not Chuy, but there was something familiar . . .

The rider sat there for another three or four minutes, then spurred his horse on out of the wash. Two others came into view, and one of them was Chuy. Matt recognized the first one now—that squint-eyed bastard who had jumped him in the brush the morning after he had crossed over into Chihuahua, the one who had challenged him in the *cantina* at Río Seco. The one Matt had kicked in the throat.

The three men rode at a walk along the hoofprints, Chuy and Squint-eye and some kind of Indian. The Indian's clubbed black hair was bound with a red rag. He wore a dirty white shirt with tails that hung down almost to the knees. There was a breech-clout under the shirt tails, and his knee-length moccasins had turned-up toes. He rode a bareback buckskin pony and carried a single-shot carbine. Squint-eye and Chuy had repeating carbines.

That's an Apache, Matt thought, an' I better watch him closer'n anybody!

Chuy said something and waved his arm. Matt could not

make out the words. The arm-wave seemed to be an order to spread out, but the Apache shook his head and pointed at the double line of hoofprints, the marks of Pecas and the gray horse.

Matt did not know how far his Spencer carbines would shoot flat. Maybe a hundred yards, and after that the slug would arc like a rainbow. He took one of them and raised the sight vane, and slid the aperture up to the hundred-yard line, then looked behind, up the slope to the upper end of the *mesa,* but it was much too soon to expect Paco.

The riders stopped where Matt had put Trini on the stallion. It was not more than ninety yards, and Matt could hear the voices carrying clear on the still air.

"Come on," Chuy was saying, "they got away because of your stupid shot there at the river! We'll go on to the ranch."

Squint-eye answered, "His horse stepped in a hole just as I fired."

"Well, come on!" Chuy ordered. He gathered his reins and his horse moved, partially hiding Squint-eye and the Apache.

The Apache said, "One horse go. Stallion go. Gray horse turn here." He pointed with his lantern jaw, up the little *arroyo.*

Matt eased back the hammer of the Spencer and pushed the muzzle out over the rock. He caught the Indian's head in the rear sight, moved the front blade into line, and fired. Chuy's horse went down in a heap as though its feet had been jerked from under it. Squint-eye yelled and yanked his mount sideways and drove in the spurs. The Apache slid down and sprinted up the little *arroyo* toward Matt and was gone like a flitting shadow. Chuy scrambled behind the dead horse and made himself small.

Matt cursed the Spencer, which had dropped the bullet inches lower than he had aimed, and jerked in another shell. At least, the hand squeeze and the recoil had not hurt too much.

Squint-eye had gone back over the edge of the wash and halfway across the flat to the river. Now he stopped to look back, and began a wide circle to get behind rocks three hundred yards away. Matt watched him ride behind the rocks and thought he dismounted, but could not be sure. Matt looked down the *arroyo* past the dead gray horse, but could see nothing of the Apache. The Apache's pony had run a few steps, and was grazing unperturbed.

There was a blossom of smoke from Squint-eye's rocks and the flat, slapping sound of the shot. Matt did not know where the bullet had gone, but he ducked behind his rocks.

He studied the *arroyo* below, every stone, every leaf shadow, every grain of sand, almost, and could not see the Apache. It began to worry him more than anything else. He could hear no hoofbeats on the road. Trini must be at the ranch by now. A lizard shot like a streak of green light from under a patch of *nopal* which leaned over the little *arroyo*, raced thirty feet, climbed a flat rock and pushed up and down on its forearms. Matt fired into the shadow of the *nopal*. The Apache leaped to his feet, pitched forward and rolled down into the *arroyo*. Blood spouted from his throat while the dust settled. Matt levered in a fresh cartridge.

Chuy's head popped up behind his dead horse, and Matt fired hastily and heard the slug slap into horseflesh. On the far edge of the flat, Squint-eye was banging away, wasting cartridges. Matt was not much concerned about him. Silence settled.

Behind the horse, Chuy's foot showed. There was not much room there for a man to hide. Matt aimed at the foot and, remembering how his first shot had struck low, held high and squeezed the trigger. The carbine bucked and spewed rolling smoke. Chuy squawked, and the smoke drifted away.

Never touched him! If I had that Sharps, he wouldn't have that foot!

He began to taunt Chuy.

"Stand up, Chuy, stand up, little boy! You know, real brave! That's how you like it, isn't it? Just you and me, and I'll blow your head off, you murdering pimp!"

He waited.

Chuy did not move. No inch of him showed. The Indian's pony had flung its head up at the sound of the shot and trotted fifty yards and was again peacefully grazing.

Matt put two cartridges into the magazine of the Spencer and waited a long time, and heard at last the faraway roll of galloping hoofs on the road. The sound grew louder and kept coming, and then stopped.

Paco's turning off the road like I wanted, he thought, and he's makin' his way to the far end of the *mesa*. Chuy may try for him if he shows himself.

He drew the revolver and cocked it and laid it beside himself. Across the flat, Squint-eye tried another shot. It was too far, and the bullet struck somewhere to one side and low.

Then Matt heard feet running down the slope behind him. He turned his head, trying to locate Paco. Chuy stood up behind the horse and fired over Matt's head—three fast shots from his revolver, and turned and ran away.

Matt fired three times at Chuy's running figure, and saw each slug kick up dirt behind him, short. He tried once more, but the hammer fell on a faulty cartridge. Matt swore savagely and slammed the lever forward and back and knew it was too late.

He heard Paco stumble and regain his footing and keep running. He stumbled again and fell and slid behind Matt, and pushed the Sharps buffalo gun under his arm. Matt did not look at him, but dropped flat behind the rocks and watched Chuy run behind a big boulder, a full two hundred yards away. Paco coughed and pushed the cartridge bag between his arms.

Matt threw the lever forward and saw the big cartridge with its 125 grains of powder and 525 grains of snub-nosed lead.

"Now!" he whispered. "Now, Medina, you Goddamn gunslinger!" He pushed the sixteen pounds of rifle over the rock and cuddled the stock to his cheek.

Then, not Paco, but Trini put an arm across his shoulder and said, between great, sobbing intakes of breath, "Mateo . . . ?" Her voice was querulous and small, like a little girl's.

Matt flung her arm off impatiently and untied the cartridge bag and dumped a handful of cartridges on the ground. There was no time to ask about Paco—the main thing was —he had the Sharps!

Squint-eye fired again from the far rocks. The slug scattered gravel ten feet to Matt's right. Better do something about him, too. He might get lucky!

Matt studied the rocks from which Squint-eye was firing. About three hundred yards, maybe a little more. He raised the tang of the rear sight, loosened the aperture disc and set it for three hundred yards and tightened the thumb screw. He checked to see that the sight drift was centered —no need to shift it since there was no wind. Then he held steady on a black blot of shadow under two rocks that leaned together, and squeezed off the shot. Its blast was shocking, after the spiteful cracking of the carbines. He saw the dirt burst up just below his aiming point. Just a little short! His right arm began to ache, and the hand trembled.

He reloaded and set the elevation for 305 yards and said, "Watch for Chuy. He's behind the big rock to the left, about two hundred *varas*."

Trini did not answer. He lined up again on the blot of shadow at the base of the distant rocks, and concentrated on squeezing his trembling hand together slowly and steadily. The recoil shoved hard and a jolt of pain tore at his arm. He heard the big slug scream off rock. Squint-eye's horse broke from behind the rocks and went across the flat like a jack rabbit running scared.

Trini coughed. She asked, "Mateo, do you love me? You never said you loved me." It might have been the ringing in his ears, but Matt could hardly understand her.

He snarled at her. "For God's sake! Look for Chuy!"

Trini put her arm over his shoulder again and pressed close to his side. "Your Cheyenne bitch," she said, "she wouldn't have got the gun like Trini. She wouldn't have come . . ."

Her voice trailed off, and Matt felt the sticky, warm wetness seeping through the *camisa* onto his ribs. When he turned and looked at her, her eyes were open, there was a thin thread of blood from the corner of her mouth, and a great, obscene stain of it on her blouse. She was dead.

Hastily, Matt looked away. He laid the Sharps down and mechanically massaged the ache that was his right forearm, but he did not feel the ache. He did not feel anything. He could not make himself look at Trini again.

The stillness was so absolute that he heard the click of the Indian pony's hoof against a stone, almost as far away as the rocks behind which Chuy lay. Almost without interest, he watched Chuy lift his head cautiously above the rock and stare toward him.

Matt shook his head and rubbed his eyes with the heel of his hand.

Rage began to rise in him like a slow tide. His hand shook as he loosened the thumb screw and set the aperture down to the two-hundred-yard line and tightened the screw. He stretched out full length, and felt Trini's arm slide from his shoulder and drop to the ground with a small thump. He moved away a little so he was not touching her, and took his time settling the rifle solidly on a rock. He propped his elbows comfortably and wiggled his hips and feet into place, and aimed at the rocks where Chuy hid. He began to feel the ache in the right arm, but paid no attention. His first shot raised a fountain of earth beside the big rock. He reloaded mechanically, shifted the muzzle a quarter of an inch and squeezed off the shot. Earth spouted up at the other corner of the rock, just where it rested on the ground. Chuy yelled something, but Matt did not try to understand him.

He had just reloaded and was trying to see if there was an opening between the heaped boulders, any hole he could put a slug through, when Chuy's head rose quickly into sight and his arm waved. Matt fired, and the head was down before the slug got there. The bullet ricocheted and wailed off, and a gray puff of rock dust blossomed from the top of the boulder, exactly where Chuy's head had been.

Chuy's shout came faintly—Matt barely heard it through the ringing of his ears—"*Gringo!* Stop!"

Matt saw a little hole between the rocks, low, about knee-high off the ground, about the size of a man's hand, and he put a shot through it without touching the sides. Chuy scrambled into view on hands and knees, then whirled and dived back behind the rocks. He was shouting something unintelligible.

Matt studied stones and rocks near Chuy's refuge, looking for some way of bouncing a ricochet behind the pile of boulders. He could see nothing that offered a means of actually hitting Chuy, but there was one smooth, imbedded stone that might bend one pretty close.

He opened the breech and shoved in a fresh cartridge and flexed his fingers and saw the bead of the front sight in the aperture, with the stone behind it. He held his breath and fired. The stone jumped and settled back, and Chuy screamed, "Stop! Stop shooting!"

Matt reloaded.

Chuy's carbine came flying from behind the rocks, whirling end-over-end, and fell in plain sight.

"Stop! See, I throw away my rifle!"

Matt's shot smashed the carbine and moved it three feet. He reached for the cartridge bag, dumped all the bright cartridges on the ground, and reloaded.

"I will go back!" Chuy shouted. "I renounce the horse! I will go back and not cross the river again!"

Matt aimed again at the little hole he had shot through before.

Chuy threw his revolver out.

"I am unarmed!" he screamed. "You will not kill! Not when I am unarmed!"

Matt put the shot through the hole, and Chuy scurried into view and ran back again.

"I am coming out! I trust you! I am going back across the river!"

Matt reloaded.

Chuy thrust both hands up into view. "Can I come out? Can I go?" His shouting voice rose to falsetto.

Matt centered the Sharps on Chuy's right hand and began the slow trigger squeeze. The recoil hammered his shoulder.

Chuy shrieked and came stumbling into view. He went to his knees, got up, ran a few steps and fell. He rose to his knees. His left hand clutched his right wrist, and on the wrist the gun hand was nothing but a pulp, a smashed wreck of a hand. He fell over on his back. His heels drummed on the ground and moved his legs in a slow circle around the pivot of his head.

Matt shoved a cartridge into the breech of the Sharps and sat up. He propped his elbows on his knees and aimed, but held his fire. The gunfighter began to crawl for the shelter of his rock, but gave it up and lay face down, clutching his wrist and moaning.

Presently, Matt laid the Sharps down and reached back blindly to find Trini's hand. He put the palm against his face and held it there. He tried to make himself believe she was better off this way. I'd never have stuck with her, he thought, and hated himself because it was true.

Squint-eye cautiously raised his head into view, then his hands. He yelled, "Let me go, eh, *gringo*? It was all Chuy! He gave the orders!"

When Matt did not reply, Squint-eye stepped hesitantly from behind the boulders and stood ready to dive back if Matt should move. Matt stared at him dull-eyed. When Squint-eye started to walk to the Indian's horse, Matt could hear the crunch of his *guaraches* on the gravel. The horse moved a few steps, but allowed itself to be caught. Squint-eye led it to Chuy.

Chuy propped himself on his elbow. "Tie my wrist," he said, "then get me on the horse."

"You will not begrudge me your fine revolver, eh, Chuy? You have no use for it, having no gun hand."

He looked at Matt and raised his voice. "You permit, *gringo*? It is a better gun than my old cap-and-ball."

Matt said nothing. Squint-eye picked up Chuy's revolver, unbuckled Chuy's cartridge belt and jerked. Chuy screamed as the pull of the belt rolled him over. Squint-eye called again, "I am not foolish enough to try the hand gun against you, *gringo!* Be reassured!" He examined the Colt revolver, spun the cylinder, checked the loads, and shot Chuy in the head.

He buckled on the belt, mounted the horse, and kicked its ribs. It began to trot toward the river.

Matt shot him off the horse. He rolled twice and lay sprawled, staring up at the sky.

In half an hour Paco came, riding the mule. He rode down the *mesa* top the way Trini had come. He had a *machete* in his hand.

He dismounted and dropped the reins and put a stone on them, then came to sit beside Matt and put a hand on his shoulder. He did not speak.

After a while, Matt asked, "Have you got a handkerchief?"

Paco took the sweat cloth from around his neck, and Matt gently wiped the blood from Trini's mouth and closed her staring eyes. He laid his jacket over her blood-stained body and smoothed the tangled hair back on the small, shining head. He looked up at Paco and said, "A favor, brother. Will you go back and get a shovel, and my Navajo blanket?"

"The blanket is clean," Paco said. "Ana washed it."

He started to walk to the mule, then turned and said, "When the girl came, I knew the horse, so I got the rifle and cartridge bag when she said you needed them. I told her to dismount, but she snatched the rifle and the bag from my hand and yelled at the horse. It jumped and knocked me down. She rode away fast. The mule was hard to catch, or I might have got here in time."

"With a *machete*," Matt said.

"The stallion is tied in the brush at the upper end of the *mesa*," Paco explained. "I think she was afraid it would be shot, so she tied it there. Is that Chuy by the rock?"

"Yes, and his Apache in the *arroyo,* and one of his as-sassins farther on," Matt replied. "And Lázaro by a cave in Chihuahua."

Paco rode away. Matt sat holding Trini's hand and staring out over the flat toward the river.

An hour later, Paco returned with the shovel and the Navajo blanket. He said, "Let me do it, brother!"

"Thanks, Paco," Matt said. "I'll manage. You go on back."

Chapter 18

THE EVENINGS were the same as before under the *ramada,* with the heat of the day still held by the earth floor and the adobe walls of the house, and the stars popping out and a soft breeze bringing relief. The children played and quarreled in the blue dusk. Ana lay stretched in the ham-mock while Eduardo nursed fiercely and noisily and the *mezcal* jug passed back and forth between Paco and Matt. Once the tale had been told, no one spoke of Lázaro or Chuy or Trini. But more often than not, Matt kept at the *mezcal* until the jug was empty, and slept in a stupor on the dirt floor.

Although he knew that Paco was waiting for him to speak about the horse-raising venture, he was not ready; and the plan held less and less interest for Matt. It now seemed like a trap to tie him down to a house and a small ranch. He felt guilty about it—it would mean everything to Paco—the difference between grinding toil in the cornfields just to scratch out a precarious subsistence, and the life of a man who raised fine horses and made a good living and was respected. Well, he thought, let it rest a while. I won't think about it now. How's the *mezcal* jug? Empty again? Better go into town.

The whiskers were gone. He had saved only a small mustache. His clothing was new and clean—a flannel shirt, wool pants, a duck jacket, a low-crowned black hat with a three-inch brim, flat-heeled, mule-ear boots. The broken arm had healed a little crooked but it worked all right. The bullet gouge across his shoulder was now only a purple welt.

Occasionally he rode into Ojo Prieto and did his drinking at Daggett's saloon.

He saw Becker, the marshal, either on the plaza or in the saloon almost every time he went to town. Several times, Becker started a conversation in friendly enough fashion, but soon his need to justify himself, to be the big, tough town marshal, would assert itself, and his remarks would become more and more challenging, verging on insult. At considerable strain on his self-control, Matt answered mildly until he could walk away or some interruption occurred. That day when Chuy had tried to bait him into suicide, when he, Matt, had shoved the marshal down the street with the muzzle of the Sharps, seemed to rankle, to irritate Becker like a pebble in a boot. Matt wished to God these gunmen didn't have to keep proving something!

And one night, pushed beyond silent anger by some remark of Becker's, he said, evenly enough, "Do me a favor, will you? Keep away from me! Just quit baitin' me! I'll say, right here in front of everybody, you're a better man than I am. That what you want? An' I won't pack a six-gun an' I won't tangle with you in no even-break gunfight. Figure I'm yellow, if you like it that way!"

He took his glass from the bar and walked to his accustomed table in the rear. Becker made some remark that Matt did not catch. Several men at the bar laughed.

Matt got drunk and stayed until Daggett pushed him out the door, but the liquor didn't do anything for him but make his head feel ready to burst in the morning, like a poisoned wolf.

It was September, but it seemed only last week that he had lain there on that *mesa* with the Sharps bucking against his shoulder and Chuy shrieking and rolling on the ground. And Trini lying beside him and pleading to be told he loved her while her life ran out. He got the jug and went to lie in the hammock. Ana looked at him big-eyed and sad, but never reproached him for his rudeness and surliness. Paco went stolidly about his business of hoeing corn and *chilis* and now, not even his eyes asked questions about raising colts.

It was time he got all this business out of his head—Trini and Wo Ista—and straightened himself out. He shook the jug. It was empty. He got out of the hammock to get the other from the hole by the well, and heard a horse walking across the plank bridge.

Swiftly, he snatched the Sharps from where it leaned against a *ramada* post and loaded it.

Karl Koch came riding over the hill on a big Morgan gelding, a bay with black points. Matt laid the Sharps in the hammock and ran to meet him. He dragged him from the saddle and the two went into a back-pounding, hollering dance. Karl was drunker than Matt, who had not really got a start. His pint bottle fell out of his shirt and broke, and the dance stopped abruptly.

"Climb up behind, Matt, you ol' squaw man! We'll go back to town for another, at that Daggett's deadfall, that bartender's, he's the one told me how to git here!"

"I'll get my horse!" Matt grinned. "The one you was gonna kill me over at 'Dobe Walls, or me you, I forget which!"

Townspeople scattered like windblown leaves as the bay and the spotted stallion charged across the plaza and made a rump-sliding stop at the hitchrack in front of Daggett's.

Inside, Matt stood the Sharps in the corner, but Koch laid his on the bar.

Daggett eyed it and said, "Friend, stand it alongside Matt's, will you? Marshal don't like it, people carryin' them cannons in town."

"Tell the marshal to shove it up his *culo*!" Koch roared. "How's that for Spick lingo, Matt! Learned it off a little Mex gal in Santa Fe. *Culo!* It means—"

"I know what it means," Matt laughed. "Daggett, bring us a bottle to that back table."

Koch lugged the big Sharps along and laid it on the table. He sprawled in a chair and yelled, "Hurry it up, grampa! We gonna do some howlin'!"

Daggett scowled and brought the bottle and two smeared glasses and went back behind the bar. Several cattlemen stood at the bar and eyed Matt and Koch with stiff-faced disapproval. Koch gave them a bold-eyed stare and poured whisky. For all his hilarity, his hand was steady, and he spilled not a drop.

He and Matt slugged down the drinks. Koch blew loudly and fanned his face. "Whoo-eee! That's straight out of some cougar's kidneys! Ain't even cooled off yet. Hey, Matt, we're goin' to Californy! I come down to get you!"

"Californy? What the hell for?"

"Hell, I don't know! Buffalo huntin's all done. Army's keepin' people out of that Injun grounds south of the Arkansas, an' there ain't any nowheres else."

California sounded pretty good to Matt. He poured another drink.

Koch said, "You know, nice warm weather, dig gold, pretty little senyoreeters, all that! Some of them fellers, you know, they come to New Mexico durin' the war, with that Californy Battalion or something. Some of them's in the Fourth Cavalry. I been talkin' to 'em."

"Speakin' of cavalry," Matt said, "did they come an' get you boys out of 'Dobe Walls after me an' Buff lit out?"

"Oh, sure. We hadda stay around two months, with them Comanch' pot-shootin' at us. They never did hit nobody. We run a little short of water, but there was plenty of liquor in Hanrahan's an' the store was full of stuff to eat. Then Lieutenant Baldwin, Frank Baldwin, you know him?"

"Yeah," Matt said. "Met him at Dodge one time."

"Well, he brought some troopers down an' took us out. 'Escorted,' he said. He give us plain hell, you'd'a' thought they was gonna hang us when they got us back."

"What'd they do to you?" Matt asked, and reached for the bottle.

"Nothin'!" Koch replied, and guffawed. "The colonel, he give us a lecture an' let us go. Lot of them officers, they think killin' off the buffalo is a good thing. Makes the Injuns be nice boys when they ain't got no more food or hides for lodges an' such. Hey, I seen ol' Buff Akins, not two weeks ago."

"Where's he at?" Matt asked.

"Well, after we got out of 'Dobe Walls I joined up with the Fourth Cavalry, civilian scout. Colonel Mackenzie's runnin' it now. There was seven troops of us messin' around in them canyons by Red River. There's a lot of Comanch' an' Kiowas an' a few Southern Cheyenne prowlin' around in there. *Was,* that is! We really busted up them camps. Hit the biggest one just at daylight. They come out of the lodges, some of them naked, squaws, bucks, kids, everybody, hollerin' an' yippin' an' tryin' to put up a fight. It was quite a set-to for a while. Only some scattered bands

got away, an' most of 'em didn't have no guns nor horses.
They'll have to come in to the reservations 'fore winter."

"You reco'nize any of the Cheyennes?" Matt asked, half
hoping . . . but Stone Calf and Wo Ista were Northern
Cheyennes—not much chance—still . . .

Someone was standing by the table. Matt looked up at
Becker, the fancy marshal.

Becker said angrily, "Goddamn it! I've told you fellows!"
His hand went toward Koch's rifle, lying on the table in
a slop of spilled whisky. Koch grasped the stock and swung
the rifle across the table and cocked it as it swung. It
knocked a glass over and stopped in line with Becker's
groin.

Becker put his fists on his hips. "If you wanta bring them
buffalo guns into town, leave 'em at the bar," he ordered.

"Uh-uh!" Koch was smiling. "Not me."

"How long you gonna be in town?" Becker demanded.

"Thinking of settlin' down here," Koch replied.

Matt said, "We're goin' away, both of us, tomorrow. So
don't do no horsin' around!"

"Best news I heard since I come here," Becker said. He
went to the bar, where the cattlemen made room for him
and Daggett had his drink poured.

The marshal swallowed his drink, then put his back to
the bar and his elbows on it. He cleared his throat. Men
nearby stopped talking and gave him respectful attention.

"Gents," he said, "that smugglin' bastard Chuy Medina
got himself killed. I got ways of gettin' the news. Somebody
beat me to it, down by Matt Fletcher's ranch a couple
months ago."

Koch wasn't listening. He belched sonorously and said,
"Matt—"

Matt snarled at him, "Shut up!"

Becker swaggered across the room and stood facing Matt.
"Yeh," he went on, "Chuy got himself shot in the head.
The *back* of the head! There was a dead Apache in a gulch,
an' a Mex'can shot with a buffalo gun. The size hole in him,
it *had* to be a buffalo gun. *He* got it in the back, too. Good
job of dry-gulchin', huh, Fletcher? Buffalo hunter style all
the way, from a stand."

Slowly Matt stood up and pushed the chair back.

Becker backed up a step and hung his hand by the grip
of his Colt.

Matt whipped the skinning knife from the Cheyenne sheath at his hip. The point was against Becker's belly. Becker kept his eyes on Matt's and began to back up. Matt crowded him.

Behind Matt, Koch said cheerfully, "Steady now, everybody!"

The marshal's back was against the bar.

Matt said, "Chuy spit in your eye an' made you like it. I'm gonna do the same." He did.

Becker's face went brick red, but he made no move.

Matt eased the knife point slowly down along Becker's belly until it came against the gun belt. He ripped the knife down and outward. The severed belt and the holstered gun thumped on the floor.

"Turn around! Step out here and turn around!"

Becker stepped away from the bar and started to turn and Matt kicked him as hard as he could swing his foot. The marshal stumbled forward and Matt followed and kicked him again and again until he ran through the doorway into the dusk of the plaza.

Matt took his rifle from the corner and said, "Come on, Karl."

Koch corked the whisky bottle and put it into his shirt, and the two walked out to their horses and mounted while the babbling broke out behind them.

Well out from the town, Koch stopped his horse and got the bottle out of his shirt. They both drank.

Koch said, "What was that ruckus all about?"

"I'll tell you some day, Karl. I got a couple of things to settle at the house, then we can start. Californy sounds good to me."

A little later, as the horses walked in step with the long shadows cast by the rising moon, Koch stopped again.

"By God, Matt, I was just goin' to tell you, when that marshal come up to the table. About Buff Akins. He was with a band of Cheyennes when we jumped that camp by Red River. He stuck with 'em, too. They got away, just six, seven of 'em in that bunch. Mackenzie set me to tracin' 'em, an' I caught up with 'em 'cause they only had two ponies. Ol' Buff, he wasn't friendly. He was lookin' at me down the barrel of that ol' percussion gun, peekin' out of some bushes. I sure was surprised to see him. Well, here's what's gonna get you, Matt—he told me if I was to see you, I should give you a message."

Koch took a gulping swallow of whisky and put the bottle back in his shirt.

"While we was palaverin'," Koch resumed, "them Injuns showed theirselves. An' this is gonna get you, Matt! That Cheyenne squaw was there, you know? The one you was so hot after, that time? She looked a little pot-bellied to me, too. Guess you really got to her, didn't you, you ol' stud horse!"

Something lifted from Matt. He felt that he might float off the stallion's back.

"What'd Buff say?"

"That ol' bastard's crazy," Koch said. "Turnin' against his own people that way. He'd've shot me, if I'd've made a wrong move. Said he would if I followed 'em, too."

"What did he say!" Matt yelled, and both horses jumped.

"What the hell's the matter with you!" Koch inquired petulantly. "He said to ask you if you remember the first lodge you set up in the aspens by a creek somewheres up in the Bighorns—I forget where he said. Said ask you if you remember how to get there."

Matt slacked the rein and Pecas began to trot. Then Matt pulled him up and turned back to Koch.

"He say anything else?" he asked.

"Yeah. He said tell you all the Cheyennes had it that *I* was the one shot that buck, the one shoved the lance into Billy Tyler's belly. Said he told 'em so, that he was there in the soddy with me and you, an' he seen me do it, an' they all believe him. Crazy ol' coot! Who cares who shot him! Then he said I better git, 'cause that girl, that Buffalo Woman, was tryin' to borrow his gun to shoot me, 'cause that buck was her brother!"

"Karl, I ain't goin' to Californy," Matt said, and slacked the rein. Pecas started to trot again.

"Matt! Hey, wait!" Matt heard the thump of Koch's heels against the Morgan's ribs.

"Go on back, Karl!" Matt shouted over his shoulder. He leaned forward and told the spotted stallion to run. Behind him, Koch began to curse. His voice faded as Matt hit the Appaloosa down the hind leg with the *romal*. The last Matt heard of him was profane imprecation.

There was no light in the house, but Paco spoke to him as soon as he dismounted.

"Light the lamp, will you, brother?" Matt asked.

Lamp light flared from the doorway and he went inside. Ana turned the wick up and looked at him questioningly.

Matt said. "Some news came and I am leaving right away."

Paco's shoulders slumped a little, but he asked no questions.

"Sister," Matt said to Ana, "do me the favor of getting my clothes together. And bring the cartridges for the big gun, and the bullet mold. And I need paper and a pen, as a favor."

"Your father had a pen and a tablet of paper," she said. "I will get them."

Matt turned to Paco. "How much money is left?"

"Well," Paco said, "you took a hundred dollars when you went into Mexico, and since you have come back, those trips into town . . ."

"Never mind, Paco. Will you get it, please?"

Paco went out, and Ana brought the pen and a bottle of ink and the writing pad.

Matt began the letter, with the lines running down in a slant. Paco came in with the can of gold pieces which had been buried by the well. Matt signed his name to the paper with a flourish and a splutter of ink spatters.

The writing was in English, with the Spanish translation appended. It read:

13th September, 1874

I give my ranch to Francisco Juan Bautista Gómez (his nickname is Paco) for him to keep it or sell it or do anything he wants to.

Matthew Frederick Fletcher

He read it aloud, and Paco said, "No, Mateo! You must not—"

Matt said, "Brother, it is what I want to do. Now, count out five hundred dollars of the money."

One by one, the coins clinked on the table.

"The rest is yours," Matt said, "to buy those mares. You will have to buy a stud, too, because I am taking the Appaloosa."

Paco's protests were sincere, but Matt would not listen. He had Ana find the moneybelt. He put the five hundred dollars in it and tied it around his waist against the skin.

"Get something for the children," he said, "something as a gift from Tío Mateo. And tell Tomás I am sorry not to say goodbye to him. Paco, please fill a saddle bag with corn. And if there is a blanket? I am sorry I lost the *serape* you gave me."

Ana brought the best blanket she owned and went out to tie it behind the cantle.

"This news," Paco said, "it is urgent, I see that. But tell me for my satisfaction, is it bad news or good news?"

"It is good news, Paco."

"And will you come back, brother?"

"No, Paco."

At the top of the hill, just as he started down, he looked back and saw the silhouettes in the doorway.

Pecas went down the hill and trotted across the bridge. He turned into the road for Ojo Prieto.

Matt leaned and patted the strong stallion neck and whispered into the split ear, "Not this time, Pecas! Do you think you could run a little?"

He squeezed with his left knee. The Appaloosa swerved to the right, went off the road and stretched out and began to run.